MIDDLE GROUND

For Piet

URSULA ZILINSKY

MIDDLE GROUND

First published in 1968 in the USA by J.B. Lippincott
This edition and introduction first published as a Gay Modern
Classic in March 1987 by GMP Publishers Ltd, PO Box 247,
London N15 6RW

British Library Cataloguing in Publication Data

Zilinsky, Ursula
    Middle ground.
    I. Title
    813'.54 [F]   PS3576.I46

    ISBN 0-85449-056-6

The lines quoted from "When first my way to fair I look" are
from *The Collected Poems of A.E. Housman*; copyright 1922 by
Holt, Rinehart and Winston, Inc; copyright 1950 by Barclays
Bank Ltd.; reprinted by permission of Holt, Rinehart and
Winston, Inc., Messrs. Jonathan Cape Ltd. publishers of A.E.
Housman's *Collected Poems*, and the Society of Authors as the
literary representative of the Estate of the late A.E. Housman.
The passage quoted from "Spiv Song" comes from *The Colour
as Naked* by Patrick Anderson, reprinted by permission of the
Canadian publishers, McClelland and Stewart Limited, Toron-
to.

Printed by the Guernsey Press, Guernsey, C.I.

INTRODUCTION

Middle Ground was first published in the United States in 1968 – at the height of the Vietnam war. It is a heartfelt plea for peace by a writer who knows the devastations of war at first hand. Ursula Zilinsky, like the central character in her novel, was separated from her family and spent much of her early life in a Europe at war. She emigrated to the USA in 1949.

The novel achieved modest sales, was reprinted in a paperback edition in 1970, and was bought as a film property, though the film was never made. A British edition was well received by critics and readers. Nevertheless, the book has been out of print for well over a decade. It was one of those books that has the misfortune to appear at the wrong time. In 1968 the Gay Liberation movement was still in the future. There was no gay press apart from small newsletters with very limited circulation and a few muscle glossies with little intellectual content. The network of communications and organizations which has grown up through the 1970s and 80s did not then exist.

Other, earlier gay novels had found their readers of course, but for the most part they were by already established authors (and could thus be assured of reviews, even if unfavourable ones) or they were tracts in which homosexuality is posed as the central "question" of the novel – a question which can never really be resolved.

In their day these books at least made their readers (of all sexual inclinations) aware that such people existed in the world. But seen from our late twentieth century position of relative freedom, what a grim conjunction of themes and images they present! The tragic endings (suicide, murder, gratuitous accidental death); the high number of invalids, missing limbs, mutilated hands, scarred faces – physical concomitants of other wounds. And the succession of confining rooms – from *Giovanni's Room* to *A Room in Chelsea Square* to the bar at the bottom of the stairs in *Advise and Consent* that must have seemed to the innocent neophyte like the doorway to Hell. From such rooms travellers fled to Morocco, to Borneo, to the Italian Islands, to the ends of the earth in search of human warmth and affection, of sex uncomplicated by guilt and the ever-present threat of punishment. They fled, or they disappeared, never to be seen again in decent society.

Middle Ground replicates these conditions, and intensifies them. The wounds become the disfiguring multiple injuries of General von

Svestrom; the confining spaces become the prison camps. Here though, the tragic ending has already occurred; the Nazi prison *is* the end of the earth, the "insurmountable roadblock lying across civilization". Here, the restrictions and damage have a clear cause – the war and despotism of twentieth century Europe. The setting seems even more appropriate today when more is known about the Nazi attempt at a systematic annihilation of homosexuals.

Heiligendorf, the camp in *Middle Ground*, is not a concentration camp but a "labour camp": "In Dachau and Buchenwald, Heiligendorf was considered a desirable place." Nor are the leading characters in the story "Pink Triangles" (prisoners interned specifically for their homosexuality). They are there because totalitarian regimes must always imprison their people; categories are merely excuses. The central relationship in the novel is between the half-Jewish teenager Tyl von Pankow, saved from the death camps by the influence of his Prussian grandfather, and Johannes von Svestrom, a war-wounded soldier over twice Tyl's age. They are two people trapped together in a nightmare devised to destroy them both (one physically, the other spiritually). Their society demands that they relate to one another only as oppressor and victim. Yet they are haunted by feelings and memories that remind them of another, forbidden relationship between man and man – love.

It seems probable that the character of General von Svestrom was based partly on an extraordinary real individual mentioned in the novel, Colonel Count Claus von Stauffenberg. The two have a great deal in common, including their similar attempts to alleviate suffering in prison camps and virtually identical multiple wounds. Like General von Svestrom, Colonel von Stauffenberg was an aristocratic officer in the German regular army, badly wounded in the North African campaign. As a young man he had been a disciple and intimate friend of the homosexual poet Stefan George, and the relationship was to influence him throughout his life. On July 20 1944 Stauffenberg carried a bomb in an attempt to assassinate the dictator. In the aftermath of the attempted coup, many officers and others were murdered by the Nazis.

The character of General von Svestrom, who disconnects the electric fence around the camp and tells the prisoners they are free to leave, would be unbelievable if it were not for one factor that becomes increasingly obvious as the story unfolds: haunted by guilt, disgust and loss, the General longs to die. It is his designated victim, the teenaged

Tyl, who intends to survive. And more than once the boy sees his overseer as a "prisoner" – as indeed he is. As for Tyl, even if on that meagre diet his "terrific shape" is not believable, his character is. It had better be – Europe was full of such tough, vulnerable orphans, and the author of *Middle Ground* was one of them.

Ursula Zilinsky depicts not only the physical horrors of totalitarianism and war but their crushing injustice, the ways they warp people and tear them from their true natures. The homosexual, of course, has already tasted something of this distortion, this enforced lovelessness. In 1968, when *Middle Ground* was first published, the atmosphere for gays was beginning to change. A revived homosexual emancipation movement was approaching its more militant phase – a phase that would bring, for the first time, some real victories. Literature forecast and reflected the change. In James Baldwin's *Tell Me How Long the Train's Been Gone*, published the same year as *Middle Ground*, the hero's young male lover accepts his sexuality openly – a great change from the threatened, enclosed feeling of the same author's *Giovanni's Room*, twelve years earlier.

So *Middle Ground* came a giant step before its time. And it made an impression on others who took part in the Gay Liberation movement as it did on me. That movement, after all, aimed at healing those wounds, opening up those confining spaces, ending the tragedies that a succession of homosexual novels had repeated and questioned, and that *Middle Ground* had showed in their final stage – as part of the tragedy of the twentieth century.

That healing is far from complete. For many, the sudden possibilities of liberation from what Baldwin called the "the male prison" could not end the centuries of isolation and self-doubt. A mechanical promiscuity, half blatant, half furtive, brought only another dead end – one that, with the onset of AIDS, became appallingly literal.

Now a post-AIDS generation must make its own assessments about sex, freedom, romance. This new edition of a unique novel addresses itself to them too. It is only appropriate that the future of Tyl and Johannes is left hopeful but undetermined. It is our future also, whatever we choose to make of it.

"It's as if a new person had been waiting for me," says Tyl, "outside the barbed wire."

Ian Young

*L'amour est injustice, mais
la justice ne suffit pas.*

Albert Camus

1

Infatuation always happens with a *semblable*.

Michael used to say, "You are my twin and my mirror."

Love can happen with anyone. The mechanics of infatuation deceived us at first. J. thought I was Gabriel. I thought, because he spoke my language in a strange place, that he was I.

Christ, what an ass! Ass Ass Aspinall, Dieter calls him, his stammer for once intentional. It's not bad, considering poor Dieter has only half his wits.

He's very nice, really, Captain Aspinall. In fact he's so nice it's embarrassing. It never seems to have occurred to him that the five of us ought rightfully to be in jail. If the Russians instead of the Americans had arrested us we'd probably be on our way to Siberia by now instead of living in some former plutocrat's mansion with steam heat and American food. Russians are very sticky about black marketeers. Especially successful ones.

At first we thought we'd clear out as soon as the adjutant's eye was off us. But Migaud said, "*Imbéciles!* You are sitting like the cat in the dairy. Stay until you have exhausted the possibilities."

Migaud deals in everything there is an overpriced demand for: bodies (for love or burial), drugs, art (real and fake), assassination. For me he is everything Aspinall would like to be. Human relations abhor a vacuum, and the fatherless find fathers everywhere.

Migaud showed me my first Matisse and my first Picasso. He has the finest private collection in Vienna, having offered to "look after" paintings for owners who, he has every reason to hope, will soon be hanged by the War Crimes Tribunal.

Migaud scolds me, feeds me, worries about my insomnia, my sex life, my laziness, is confessor, critic, and crying towel, and, if offered the right price, would sell me to the nearest butcher shop for sausage meat without a tear.

I love him for the prince behind the toad and the mind that feeds mine.

The only real drawback to staying here is that the Captain is so keen about his job. (He's supposed to repatriate us and find our families, if any.) First he discovered a disagreeable old aunt of Dieter's, and now, so help me, he's found the Rittmeister (my grandfather). I thought the Russians would have hanged the bastard for sure, or I would have given a false name.

He wrote me a very nice letter, the Rittmeister. He is living in Bonn now. Pankow—his estate in East Prussia—is a collective farm. He suggested we let bygones be bygones. Families should be together, and he is looking forward to welcoming me home.

When I explained that the Rittmeister only thought he'd get denazified more quickly with me in tow, Captain Aspinall was sad but understanding. He's a doll, really. A soldier doll with a uniform, a psychology degree, and an infinite capacity for understanding things he knows nothing about. My God, how he understands!

There's a laugh for you, Karel, the Heiligendorf Six with their private psychologist.

The Heiligendorf Six are only five now, because Karel Killian died of typhus. I could tell that to the Captain, I guess. He's always after us to tell him things.

"If you want to have a talk, I am always here."

Captain, dear Captain, Karel Killian died of typhus. And an overdose of morphine, to be perfectly frank with you. It's one of the things that keeps me awake nights.

"Oh," he'd say, "that's a shame. Was he a special friend of yours?" And he would write it in the file he keeps on us with "?homosexual" in the margin. Because he is a psychologist.

I could say, "No, my dear Captain, Karel was not ?homosexual. Karel was a Communist." But that would distress him. Captain Aspinall doesn't really mind people being ?homosexual. But Communists are a subject on which the kind Captain and my grandfather see very much eye to eye.

"What's a spiv?" I ask Captain Aspinall.
"A low-class criminal, I believe. Why do you ask?"
"Sticks and stones."

> There are plenty of friends, my man, my monster,
> For a Ganymede kid and a Housman lad,
> And plenty more you would hate to discover
> What you do for a living, my spiv, my id.

It was sent me, a half page torn from a book of poetry, by the English soldier of the other night. I am used to insulting billets-doux, but I wish he'd sent the rest of the poem. I like it.

"Come and sit by the stove," says Captain Aspinall. "Aren't you cold? That jacket of yours isn't nearly warm enough for Vienna in January."

"I'm used to being cold." He's been trying for weeks to get up the nerve to ask me why I wear an Afrika Korps tunic. I've cut off the palm tree emblem and rank badges, so he can't legitimately object to it.

"It's an Afrika Korps tunic, isn't it?"

"Yes."

"I thought so. A friend of mine was at Kasserine Pass."

"On the wrong side."

"Not in the long run."

I like him better when he bites back. But he says immediately, "I'm sorry, that was nasty and unnecessary. Tell me though, why do you of all people wear an Afrika Korps tunic?"

"Everybody wears old uniforms. You can't buy new clothes."

"You could have, easily, on the black market. I think there's something special about this one. I've noticed the way you touch it, not at all like an ordinary piece of clothing. Did it belong to someone you were fond of?"

Oh, God, Aspinall, you are a horse's ass. Don't you think I know where you're heading?

I tell him the truth. "It belonged to my uncle. He was killed at Tobruk."

It's so easy to stick in a pin and let out all the air. Too easy. There isn't any sport to it.

I find my lying face in Captain Aspinall's file. He keeps detailed files on all of us and doesn't seem to notice that he supplies most of the answers as well as the questions.

Name: Tyl von Pankow. I don't bother to lie about it. It is my most meaningless possession. The obsession others have with names is a riddle to me. Who are you? What are you called? Why do they always ask it? What does it tell them?

I am memory, a bad conscience, insomnia, your most casual, one-time lay. All these would tell part of my truth. But I say, "I am Tyl von Pankow," and it tells them nothing at all.

Age: Nineteen. Two years too many, but a lie of such long standing it feels like the truth.

Hair: Blond. Eyes: Gray. Yes, I know, Captain, I don't look it. It was only my mother, you see——. Though come to think of it she was as tow-haired and gray-eyed as any Pankow. (Americans may be here to teach us democracy, but when they say, "You don't look it," it is always meant as a compliment.)

Home address: That's a laugh. Kolkhoz something or other, Post Office Braniewo, formerly Braunsberg, East Prussia.

"I don't think that's funny, Tyl."

"You would if you knew Rittmeister von Pankow."

Parents: Dr. Rüdiger von Pankow and Franziska Maria Elie.

"Do you have any idea where they might be?"

"Dead maybe." Some chance.

Once I told the Captain that the Gestapo gave my father a choice of divorcing Franziska or keeping her company in a concentration camp. (This part is true.) Without any encouragement from me the romantic Captain then invented for himself the touching story of all those towheaded little Pankows trooping off to Buchenwald with their beautiful Jewish mama. Dear God in heaven!

Any scars or permanent marks of identification?

"Uh—yes, Captain Aspinall."

He blushes but writes it down as carefully as if it were an important telephone number. When he gets over being embarrassed he even laughs because I have to pull up my sleeve to look. I can never remember it.

January 31, 5 A.M. A long month with long nights. I'm glad this is the last. I can get through the days all right. My English is getting quite good. I'm reading *Dorian Gray*. I wish I could sleep. I used to be such a good sleeper. I never thought I'd lose the knack. Also I used to think I'd spend the rest of my life eating if I got the chance. Now I have the chance and my stomach turns over at the thought of it. It's as if a new person had been waiting for me outside the barbed wire. I've never hated anyone so much as the sleepless neurotic with the queasy appetite that is me at liberty. I miss the hungry animal I used to be; that's the truth.

The others aren't like that. They enjoy their meals. They sleep. (A good conscience is a soft pillow, my Elie grandmother used to say.) They have nightmares, of course. We all do. Captain Aspinall would love to know about those.

Captain, I dream about RAF fliers. There were eight of them originally. Colonel Weizeck said they were spies. For all I know they were. He said he would hang them unless they confessed. He used the Blitzstein boy to show them what it would be like.

One day he took three fliers and hanged two. Another he took five and hanged one. Other times he'd take them all and hang none. In the end three were left and he stopped there.

Nobody knew why. One of the fliers, whose name was Piers, killed himself later.

"Captain Aspinall, I never remember what I dream about."

"If you do, come and tell me about it. You'll find it helps."

"Sure thing, Captain. Scout's honor."

But I'll never tell you the truth, dear Captain. It's so easy shitting you I can't stop. Only you make it too easy; you take all the sport out of it. It's like what you call taking candy from a baby.

Candy. Hershey bars, chewing gum, and cigarettes. Those were the first things the Americans gave us. They turned out their pockets and handed us everything they had.

They were the first American soldiers any of us had seen. They were very different from the nice Captain. They were generous but not nice. They looked like soldiers.

I refused the Hershey bars and took only the cigarettes. It half killed me to do it. But Karel had always maintained that chocolate was for little children. Cigarettes, black bread, and black coffee constituted, according to Karel, the proper diet for a revolutionary. We hadn't been able to do much for Karel, not have a proper funeral or anything, so I refused the chocolate as a last tribute, you might say, to my friend.

The worst guards had cleared out ahead of the Americans. They rounded up the rest of them and marched them off with bayonets in their backs.

"Watch well," Franticek said to me. "If you live to be a hundred you will never have a happier day." I believed him. It wasn't till later that I cried.

My grandfather did not neglect to point out in his letter that, as he had often told us (*ad nauseam*), no good can come of eccentric and irregular behavior. Meaning my father, who had whimsically elected to be a surgeon rather than an officer, was to blame for the whole mess.

Pankows breed Prussian officers the way farmers breed pigs.

Pankows always marry the daughters of East Prussian land-owners. But the study of medicine took my father to Vienna, where he fell in love with Franziska Maria.

She was blonde and gray-eyed, she became a Lutheran to please the family (the Elies were Catholics in any case), she had a lot of money, and she was an industrious breeder. I have three younger brothers and twin sisters.

I've been told that at the time of my father's marriage the main objection to Franziska was a certain Viennese levity and a liking for jokes which fitted ill with the Rittmeister's life-is-real-life-is-earnest philosophy. My grandmother, who was only half Prussian, the other half being divided equally between England and France, was much cheered by the appearance of Franziska, and we all lived at Pankow until I was ten. That year my grandmother died in a hunting accident, my Elie grandparents expressed the wish that at least one of their grandsons should be sent to St. Pölten, a school with which they had close ties, my parents could see no reason not to humor my rich grandparents, the Rittmeister flew into a rage, and my parents moved to Berlin.

St. Pölten wasn't bad once they got used to having a Prussian in an Austrian school. I happened to be good at sports and not too scrupulous at defending myself; I was an undistinguished scholar and presently made my way into the pack that ran the school. The drawing master almost ruined me by discovering I had "talent" (he was right, too), but since I used this mainly for making caricatures of the masters I was forgiven. I suppose, after swallowing my East Prussian accent, a talent for painting seemed a small mouthful. That first year at St. Pölten wasn't a bad preparation for Heiligendorf, all told.

I always spent my holidays at Pankow to give my grandfather the opportunity to erase any Austrian taint that might have crept into my speech or opinions. I rarely spent much time in Berlin. I suppose it was hell on Jews, that last year before the war. I've got to remember that, if I want to be fair.

Shit, I don't want to be fair. The fact is they bolted and left me behind.

My father explained it carefully in a long letter. He wanted to be sure I understood. One of his Nazi patients had given him the warning that they were going to round up Franziska and her children that night. And, if he refused to divorce her, him too.

The decision, he wrote, caused them both the greatest agony, but he was sure I would understand that the welfare of the majority must always come first. It was bad luck that I was too far away to be fetched in time. They were inconsolable, but there was nothing to be done. He would of course move heaven and earth to make it possible for me to follow them to Stockholm soon. Meanwhile the Rittmeister would look after me.

The next letter came from the Rittmeister. Unlike my father's letter it was not addressed to me but to the headmaster of St. Pölten. My grandfather pledged himself to continue to pay for my education on the condition that I spend my holidays as well as the school year at St. Pölten and did not attempt to communicate with him.

My Elie grandparents had been arrested right after the *Anschluss*. I never heard from them again. They were old people; I don't suppose they survived.

Monsignor Hesbach, who was the chaplain at St. Pölten, had been a great friend of theirs. After the Rittmeister's letter he invited me to spend my holidays with him. I'd always liked him, and he had the right idea about vacations: skiing at St. Anton at Christmas, Vienna for the Easter holidays, sailing on the Wörthersee in the summer.

Gabriel, my father's younger brother, was the only member of the Pankow family who came to visit me at St. Pölten. He was twenty years younger than my father and only twelve years older than I. It never occurred to me to call him uncle.

Gabriel was my favorite relation. He was gay and handsome and debonair, he wore the black uniform of the tank corps, and I considered him the most enviable of creatures until he was burned alive in his tank at Tobruk.

His visits were brief, infrequent, and exciting. He was an officer and his time was not his own. But he never forgot. I loved him. I love him still.

In 1942, when I was on the point of moving to the senior cadet school in Mährisch-Weisskirchen, someone noticed a small detail which had at St. Pölten been tactfully overlooked.

Mother's name: Franziska Maria von Pankow, née Elie.

Oh yes, dear Captain Aspinall, families should be together.

2

A sense of proportion is not one of my virtues. Therefore the knowledge that others are more miserable than I has never afforded me consolation.

Karel, who had the experience, always maintained that compared to some of the other camps he had known Heiligendorf was a veritable spa. It was not even officially a concentration camp but was designated as a labor camp.

In a labor camp, according to Karel, while no one would question our death, should it occur, it was no one's job to cause it, either. Heiligendorf was a small place and manageable. There were no small children in the camp, no women, no terribly old or ill people.

These differences seemed to me at the time too subtle to be anything but bitterly ironic. That was of course due to lack of information. I had not seen Dachau and Buchenwald. I had never even heard of Auschwitz.

"Say what you will," Karel used to say, "Colonel Shit is a bastard, but he isn't actively vicious."

I remember hooting at that. In his passive way Colonel Weizeck, whom we all called Colonel Shit (Weizeck—*Scheissdreck;* it rhymes in German) did very well.

Karel said, "Fact. You've no one to compare him with. At least he doesn't practice skeet shooting with babies as targets. The one in Dachau did."

Fair enough. Heiligendorf was not Dachau, it was not Buchenwald. It was most especially not Auschwitz. Though if you got sick or for some other reason displeased Colonel Shit, you could quite easily be transferred there.

Heiligendorf is a small village in the mountains near Linz. The camp itself was sufficiently far from the village that the natives could say they did not know it was there.

I found out later that I was sent to Heiligendorf as a favor to my grandfather. I suppose it kept whatever conscience he had quiet.

I arrived from Mauthausen with a truckload of new prisoners. Except for me everyone was from another camp, and except for me everyone was fairly cheerful. In the world of concentration camps, Heiligendorf had a good reputation.

At Mauthausen I had submitted, with a rage so blinding that it erased fear, to having my head shaved and to a medical examination which was not designed to discover any ailment. Coming so recently from the smart-aleck world of school, I made the mistake of saying, "Are you getting your kicks?" to the medical orderly. It got me my first camp beating; very different from a parent's or schoolmaster's punishment, very different too from the sheer physical violence of an enraged fight with a contemporary. There was no rage in this and no violence. Done at leisure, quite peaceably, each blow was calculated with absolute precision to give the maximum of pain.

I was sore and stiff by the time we arrived at Heiligendorf, and in a fine fit of bad temper.

We were assigned two to a bunk. There was one blanket. It smelled of disinfectant. I told my partner he was welcome to it. He told me his name was Blitzstein. He was crying. He tried to do it quietly. I didn't pay any attention to him. I had enough on my plate.

He apologized. He said he had been at Buchenwald with his parents and had only this day been separated from them. He did not think he would ever see them again.

I said, "You never know your luck."

Two candles lit the barracks. One was shared by five young men who were in comfortable possession of a good half of the room. The other half seemed to be a kind of ghetto. At least thirty people were crowded into it. They too had one candle. A depressed-looking, beaky young man from the ghetto brought his candle over to our bunk. He said to me, "What is your name? Where are you from?"

You don't survive as a Prussian in an Austrian military school without knowing certain basic rules, the chief of which is not to get mixed up with losers. I didn't like his looks or his crowd. So I said nothing.

He shrugged and turned to the Blitzstein boy. They talked for a long time in Polish. Many of the peasants at home speak Polish, and I can understand it fairly well. I didn't try to listen. I wasn't interested.

Presently one of the card players said, "Kip down, rabbi." Blitzstein's depressed friend hunched his shoulders, blew out his candle, and went back to the crowded side of the barracks. The card players lifted up a floor board and put away their cards. The one who had spoken before said, "Quiet," and blew out his candle. It was beautifully timed. Not a minute later a guard with a German shepherd made the rounds. Barrack 4A was silent. Even Blitzstein managed to stifle his sobs.

I was curious about the five men who had been playing cards. One would think half-starved men with striped uniforms and shaven heads would all look alike. But these five were different. Blitzstein and the one they called rabbi and the rest of that crowd, they looked alike. I wanted nothing to do with them.

At midnight the guards changed. We heard their steps and mutual good nights. One of the boys from the ghetto side got up and went outside. A match flared beside my bunk. It was one of the card players, the one with the high cheekbones and narrow eyes who had been giving the orders. The shaven head suited him. He looked like a Tartar chieftain. I found him entirely reassuring.

He put out his hand and touched Blitzstein on the shoulder. "Fuck off, sheeny."

Blitzstein obeyed instantly, joining the rabbi on the ghetto side of the room. My visitor swung himself up and took Blitzstein's place. "So," he said.

During my first year at St. Pölten I had learned the value of silence. It throws the burden of the first move on the other party.

"You look good," he said. "Where are you from?"

"St. Pölten."

"Is there a camp there now?"

"Just a school."

He half grinned at that. "A nob! What's your name?"

I told him.

"I'm Karel Killian. Why are you here? Political?"

It seemed the thing to be. "Yes."

"All respect. A Red at St. Pölten."

I was not entirely sure what he was talking about, but my grandfather passionately disapproved of Communists, so it seemed a good thing to be.

"I knew the minute you walked in you weren't one of them." He looked at the ghetto.

"One of what?"

"Sheenies."

I had never heard the word before that evening, but I could guess what it meant. I said, "I am, as a matter of fact. At least half. My mother is."

He said, "Stupid. I don't mean Jews. Sheenies."

"Isn't it the same thing?"

"Not here it isn't. Look at them. Can't you pick them out? If they were all going to be hanged in the morning, they'd wait their turn and not even bite a guard on the way. And I wouldn't lift a finger to help a one of them. They deserve everything that happens to them."

"But what can they do?"

"Survive," said Karel. "It's the only thing that counts now. Outlive the Nazi bastards. How old are you?"

I added two years and said, "Sixteen."

"Where are your parents?"

I said nothing.

"Oh, sorry. Are you warm enough? I could let you have a blanket."

"I'm all right, thanks."

"How'd you get that black eye?"

I told him, proudly. He said, "You're an ass." But when he swung himself down a moment later and rejoined his group, I could see he was laughing.

The Blitzstein boy did not come back. For the rest of my stay at Heiligendorf, when I chose to have it so, my bunk was my own.

Deutschland über alles blared from the loud-speakers at the four corners of the camp. It was six o'clock; a mountain mist was in the air, promising a beautiful August day.

Karel gave instructions to the newcomers: "Wash, you filthy bastards. Make a mess and I'll kick your balls in."

The washing arrangements consisted of two taps outside the barracks. There was a latrine trench, and that was all.

The morning's activities were accompanied by marches from the loud-speakers. I thought this rather exhilarating the first morning but soon became like everyone else in camp and would, if given a choice, have infinitely preferred a daily Gestapo beating to one more march.

We assembled on the square, which was cornered by the four barracks: A, B, C, and D. A meadow sloped to the camp commander's house; a pleasant Austrian chalet, its window boxes filled with pink geraniums, its small garden bright with larkspur and carnations. When the wind blew in the right direction it made a nice change from the latrine trench.

Behind the camp commander's house, another meadow sloped to a stream. But between us and the water was the electrified barbed-wire fence. At one corner of the square was the gallows, without which, according to Karel, no camp, concentration or labor, ever managed. Ours was a simple wooden scaffolding with butcher's hooks driven into the wood. Past 4C was a small, worked-out quarry. Prisoners were sometimes made to work there, Karel said, as a punishment for offenses not grave enough to merit hanging.

We had arrived in the dark, and I had not realized until morning how beautifully Camp Heiligendorf was situated. It lay in a valley surrounded by mountains on three sides, open on the fourth with a view of farms and checkered fields sloping to the Danube. Heiligendorf consisted of a few houses and a toy church halfway up the mountainside. Past the village, poised white amid the pines, was the convent of Heiligendorf, which is considered one of the jewels of Austrian baroque. It's in all the guidebooks.

There was a news broadcast, all of it good.

"Attention!"

We stood. Somewhere behind me someone whispered, "Dear God, not that again." I do not think among so many impressions I had been aware until then of the sense of fear all around me. At this moment I could no longer imagine how I could have received any impression but that one. It filled the air.

The door to the camp commander's house opened and he stepped outside, holding a cup of coffee in his hand: a brisk, pink man smiling in the brisk morning air. His black SS uniform failed to hide a paunch. What had I expected? Frankenstein's monster? Count Dracula? I don't know. Something to match the terror that made the air unbreatheable.

Colonel Weizeck spoke with the comfortable drawl of Austria, the slurred vowels and softened consonants so unsuited to the speech of authority. He greeted the newcomers amiably, commented upon the lovely morning, said that he ran a happy camp, smiled a blue-eyed smile, and added that Camp Heiligendorf had no discipline problems. The reason for this was simple: he believed firmly in the old tenet that one picture was worth a thousand words. Therefore, for the instruction of the newcomers he would demonstrate just once what would happen to anyone who by troublemaking, escape attempts, a sullen attitude, or otherwise obstreperous behavior changed the happy tenor of Camp Heiligendorf.

A hawk hanging like a black cross in the blue sky caught his interest. Without raising his voice over the noise of the marches from the loud-speaker, he said, "Merz."

The man who stepped forward showed neither protest nor surprise. He was just a man with a striped uniform and a shaved head. I had not yet learned to judge the age of faces left bare of flesh by long starvation; I thought him old. I don't imagine he was much over thirty, really. Not many people at Heiligendorf were.

As placidly as if he were performing a daily, uninteresting task, Merz took off his striped uniform and left it neatly folded on the ground. Then he walked obediently between two guards to the posts with the butchers' hooks driven into the wood.

No one cried out, moved, protested. Two hundred of us stood silent and watched. Karel, who was next to me, briefly touched my hand; a warning to keep still. The loud-speakers played background music: "Give me your hand, your white hand, farewell, my dearest—" The Blitzstein boy retched and vomited. Colonel Weizeck did not reprimand him. He scarcely changed his smiling glance. But Blitzstein had been noticed.

Breakfast consisted of two pieces of bread, made of a mixture of sawdust and potatoes, and a brown, hot liquid called coffee. I think it was brewed from ground acorns and chicory. Karel maintained it was pure camel dung. It was so bitter it wrung the mouth, but there was plenty of it and it was hot. I found myself presently getting quite fond of it. But it was definitely an acquired taste.

Though there was a guard present and conversation was kept low, there was a good amount of talk. It contained an undercurrent of gaiety and celebration which was natural enough for survivors, but which I found sickening. To demonstrate my fine sentiments I did not touch my breakfast. Karel said, "Eat. There won't be any more food till tonight."

"I can't get it down."

"Don't be a horse's ass."

With my first bite I realized that I was very hungry. I hadn't eaten, in fact, since breakfast the day before. The only other person who seemed to have trouble swallowing was Blitzstein. He was very green. A man with a beard from another table snatched up his two pieces of bread. Blitzstein did not protest.

"Give it back," said the rabbi.

"Fuck you."

"Give it back," Karel said.

The beard put the bread on the table, turned away, and spat on the floor.

"He's a Menshevik," Karel said to me. "It always shows."

I did not answer and successfully concealed the fact that I did not know what a Menshevik was.

When we came out from breakfast, Merz was dead. One of the guard dogs was having a game, snatching at his dangling heels.

Heiligendorf supplied the work force for a munitions plant camouflaged among the pines higher up the mountain.

We piled into two trucks and were driven out the gates. The transportation was not provided from kindness, Karel explained, but because it was easier to supervise us in a confined space. In the early days of the camp the prisoners had walked to the munitions factory, and several had successfully escaped into the woods.

It was like driving through a tourist poster. I had spent several years now in Austria, but my childhood had been passed among the flat lakes and moraines of East Prussia, and I never grew accustomed to the view and to the mountains which on every side cramp the eye. All the way up the winding road one could look back to the camp.

Whoever had done the camouflage for the factory was a

genius. I didn't see it until we drove into the gate. When we jumped down from the truck, Karel said, "Is that all the shoes you brought, those sneakers?"

I explained that I had been picked up in the middle of a game of tennis with Monsignor Hesbach and had managed only to snatch up my toothbrush before being taken away.

The combination of upper-class sport and clericalism made Karel snort. He said, "Serves you right, playing tennis with a priest. I'd go barefoot while the warm weather lasts and save them for winter, if I were you. They'll be better than no shoes at all, though not much."

Someone said, "A pair of boots is worth more than Shakespeare," in an obvious burlesque of Karel. It was, I soon learned, one of his favorite statements. I think his first doubts about my being a genuine Commie grew from the fact that I did not recognize the quotation.

Two guards checked us in at the gate. "Number?"

"Pankow."

"I said number."

I pulled up my sleeve to look. The guard's fist smashed into my face.

"You're supposed to know your number, pig. You can forget your name here. You don't need a name. You are nothing but garbage, do you understand?"

My mouth was full of blood. The guard turned to check off the next prisoner. Behind his back, schoolboy habit made me stick out my tongue at him. Blood ran down my chin.

Karel slapped his hand over my mouth. "Don't do these stupid things, damn it! A beating yesterday, more trouble today, how the hell long do you think you'll last at this rate?"

"Who cares? Garbage." Talking hurt. I'd bitten my tongue.

"Damned fool. Survive. Rule number one. Stick it out. Some day they'll be the garbage again."

"Like when?"

"Never mind when. It'll happen. Here, stick with me. I'll show you what to do."

I was grateful, for the large room seemed at first only a confusion of conveyor belts and metal. The walls were sandbagged. One of the bags had a slit in its side. As we passed, Karel bent and filled both hands with the sand that had fallen out. The other members of his group did the same.

Our job at the moment, he explained, was to fill shells with gunpowder. He did not say anything about the sand. I stood at a long table between Karel and a dark-haired Frenchman whom Karel introduced as Jacques. "Jacques's slave labor," Karel explained. "He lives in the village. They have a lot of them working on the farms, but Jacques is a lazy bastard, so he volunteered for the factory. It's easier than farming anyhow. Tyl's a comrade from East Prussia, just arrived."

"Bad luck," said Jacques and shook my hand with a sandy grip. He wore ordinary, threadbare clothes. Each pocket was filled with sand. "How do you find the camp?"

"I've only been here one night. They hanged a man this morning."

"Yes, I heard. I know Weizeck. He comes into the inn at the village and plays skittles. He's very jolly and popular. The thing about him is that he really isn't vicious, just lazy. He doesn't want to be bothered with discipline, so he uses the shortest, easiest way. It's probably very effective."

"Very," Karel agreed.

I was in awe of Karel, but I found Jacques easy to talk to. I said, "The man they hanged just went. Like a bag of straw. He didn't seem frightened, even, though he must have been. It made me furious."

"A zombie," said Karel to Jacques.

"What's a zombie?" I asked.

"Someone who's given up."

"Given up what?"

"Surviving."

"Do lots of prisoners give up?"

"Yes."

"Well, really," said Jacques reasonably, "what can they do?"

"Survive," said Karel again. "It's the only thing that counts just now. Keep out of trouble, stay anonymous, never get sick, never get indifferent or lazy, don't be a coward, don't be a hero. A live Communist is better than a dead reactionary."

I recognized the quotation this time. Napoleon had held that a live scoundrel was better than a dead emperor. How, I wondered, did this square with the sand surreptitiously trickled into the gunpowder?

"What's the sand for?"

"I thought that question would be next," said Karel, apparently pleased with his new pupil. "That's Operation Fuck-up. Jacques invented it. A shell filled half with sand won't explode."

So Jacques had not volunteered for the factory because he disliked farming. I said, "If you can get hanged just to inspire discipline, where does sabotage get you? You'll be a dead Communist before you know it."

"The chances are fifty-fifty. Sabotage shortens the war."

"Huh!" This was 1942. I didn't believe it. I was hungry, and sorry for myself. But the next time I passed the sandbags on the way back from the lavatory, I too filled my hands with sand. Might as well do something.

The work was simple, repetitious, and tedious. It was also very dangerous, which was why we instead of more valuable Germans were used for it. The tedium swamped the danger, though. One rarely thought of it.

The length of our working day depended on the time of the year, since the guards liked to get us back inside the barbed wire well before dark. In August this gave us almost twelve hours to work in, with a half-hour break for lunch if we had saved half of our breakfast or the Frenchmen had scrounged stuff from their farms to share with us, which to their everlasting glory they often did.

When we checked out at night, I tried the other guard.

"Number?"

"Pankow."

He put a pencil mark on his list, said, "That's a nasty black eye you've got," and passed me through.

By the time we got back to the camp I was hungry, sore, dog-tired, and in a foul temper. Dinner did nothing to cheer me. It consisted of rotten potatoes (and not enough of those) and a paper-thin slice of mouse sausage. This was so-called not because it was made of dead mice (it contained no meat of any sort) but because of its gray, hairy appearance. There were un-limited quantities of camp coffee and, for some obscure reason, mustard. Karel informed me kindly that this was the good meal. On alternate days we had repulsive slops known as boiled vomit.

No one had removed Merz from the gallows.

They counted us once more, and our day was over. In spite of Merz dangling from the gallows, and stomach cramps, I climbed into my bunk and at once fell asleep.

A hand over my mouth made me jump in panic. It was Karel. "Shsh! Keep quiet. Do you want a smoke?"

I would rather have gone back to sleep but was too recently from the precedence and etiquette of school to say so. I recog-nized the invitation as a tribute paid not to my winning personal-ity but to my political leanings. Perhaps by preserving an enigmatic silence I would be able to keep up my end a while yet. I admired Karel tremendously and wanted terribly to become his friend.

Just outside the open door stood the guard, a dog at his heels, his shoulder propped against the wall, smoking and talking to a boy from our barracks.

"It's all right," said Karel. "Jasper's mine."

"How do you mean?"

"The guard. I blackmail him."

What, I wondered, could a Nazi guard do which would be punishable on the word of a prisoner?

"He's a queer," said Karel. "Colonel Shit hates fairies."

Like most boarding schools, St. Pölten had its scandals and

private lore. Though nothing of much interest had occurred during my four years there, memory of the most trusted senior boy in charge of the freshman dormitory was still green, not to mention the swimming coach who had won fourteen trophies for the school in spite of the fact that the only thing allegedly practiced in the bathhouse was sodomy. The trophies were appropriately known to the school as loving cups; the coach had never been caught but had gone on to become a widely publicized hero of the ski paratroops and was loyally applauded by old St. Pölten boys whenever his photogenic profile appeared in newsreels.

I said, "Who's that with him?"

"That's his boy. His name's Martin Lenz. Poor Jasper's been gone on him for three years already."

"Poor Martin Lenz, I should think."

"Oh, it's not so bad," said Karel. "You get used to it, and it all helps."

"Helps how?"

"You get easy jobs around the camp, extra smokes, no factory work, that sort of thing."

"Ugh. I'd take the factory any day."

"You've only had it one day," said Karel. "Come and meet the comrades."

Franticek Killian was Karel's brother. Paul Vocovec, an ex-labor organizer, was Franticek's and Karel's oldest friend. Dieter, the youngest member of the group, had a stammer, an eager smile, and blank eyes. His father had been a Communist journalist in Vienna; he had been killed at Dachau.

And there was Abri, Avrom Margolis, the beauty (yes, even with a shaven head and emaciated face), the special one, with the look of one of Raphael's young cardinals, Karel's aide-de-camp and court philosopher (mine now), no one's friend.

After almost four years I still know little more about any of them than this. Karel could talk the night away like Scheherazade with stories of clandestine publications, organizing strikes, and street fighting in Prague, but it was astonishing how little about himself the stories told.

Almost four years have passed, and except for Karel we are still together.

Franticek and Paul, with their endless card games, girls, and glasses of beer—why are they friends, what do they mean to do with themselves, what, if anything, do they talk about when they are alone? They must be close to thirty, both of them. Too old to keep playing cops and robbers.

I've never cared much for either of them. All I know about them after four years are the contents of their nightmares.

Dieter has accepted freedom and wealth with the same eager smile, the same empty-eyed amiability, he brought to life in the camp. What happened to his father, who was Karel's friend, in Dachau? I've never asked him. I supply him with comics and sweets as if he were a child. But he is eighteen. When the Americans found his aunt he cried. He said he did not want to leave us. He was happy with me. Happy!

And Abri? I am never comfortable with him, for he knows my secret. And how can he not hate me for it? His parents were burned alive in a synagogue in Cracow by the German occupation authorities. German soldiers locked the doors and barred the windows and set the synagogue on fire. Karel told me this, not Abri. Abri must have told Karel, though, for they did not know each other till Dachau.

How does he put up with us? Franticek and Paul, Dieter and his Captain Marvel comics, me and my voracious, indiscriminate reading. (Abri says I misuse books as a drunkard misuses drink, and that's a fair-enough description.)

I don't know, I don't know. I don't give a damn about any of them. That is the truth. I could get up and walk out on them with never a second thought. I could turn my back on the survivors. But I made my promise to Karel.

That first night in camp we smoked two cigarettes Jacques had given Karel, and we talked. Everyone spoke German. They twisted it into Russian sentence structures, added Polish curses and Yiddish jokes, but the pidgin of the camps was the language of the jailers. This seems to have been true everywhere.

No one questioned my credentials. I made an effort to do my smoking without coughing. I had never smoked before except experimentally. Of the two silly habits I acquired in camp this was the more stupid, since cigarettes were so hard to come by.

Once, when a guard—not Jasper—passed outside, Karel said, "Blow out the candle, rabbi."

I asked, "Is he really a rabbi?"

Abri turned his head, startled. "Did you tell Karel you were a Jew?"

"I am, on my mother's side. She was called Franziska Elie."

"It sounds all right. Haven't you ever seen a proper rabbi?"

"No. I never knew any Jews at all. I don't think there were any at Pankow, and there certainly weren't any at St. Pölten."

"That explains it. Listen, Tyl, that shit over there is as much a rabbi as Dieter is Winston Churchill. I don't know how he got the name. Probably the way people who are seven feet tall get called Shorty."

"The prisoners were told to dig a deep hole," said Karel. I must have dozed off. "Then they were ordered to jump into it. The guards turned the water hoses on them. It was Sunday afternoon and they were bored. When the water got high and the prisoners tried to climb out, the guards pushed them back. One woman held her small son above the water even after it had risen over her head. He was the last one alive. The guards fished him out and dried him off and dressed him. They kept him in the guardhouse after that as a kind of mascot and were always very good to him."

Abri said, "She would have been a better mother if she had let him drown."

Though I fell asleep again a moment later I know I did not dream this.

3

A first week passes quickly, even on Devil's Island, probably. The camp was new, frightening, exciting: a place of possibilities, bad ones, mostly, but still unexplored. But six days of work that is dangerous and always the same and one day at the camp, dangerous and always the same, are quickly learned by heart, and after that anything—a fly in the coffee, a beating, a hanging—anything is welcome.

We did not work on Sundays because the man who owned the munitions plant was a devout Catholic. "A typical goyim twist," said Abri, teasing Karel. But all he got for it was a long lecture on the evils of private ownership of means of production.

It had not taken Karel long to discover that my background as a Communist left much to be desired. Far from being annoyed by this, Karel was pleased. It showed, he said, that, though coming from a totally fucked-up family, I had the right instincts. As for my education, he could easily take care of that.

During the nighttime hours of Jasper's guard duty and on those long hungry Sundays, lying on my bunk, smoking Jacques's cigarettes, Karel presented me with a detailed history of the rise of communism. His lectures were frequently punctuated by a sharp-knuckled rap over the ear. "Wake up, you Prussian brat!"

"I wasn't asleep, Karel. I can listen better with my eyes shut."

"Oh, yeah? What was I saying?"

As all schoolboys know, there is a trick to this. "MTS. Machine Tractor Stations." All one does is repeat the last words.

Other times I was in trouble. The fine points of the Bukharin-Preobrazhensky debates, the endless disagreements between Stalin and Trotsky, the subtle difference between a sovkhoz and a kolkhoz were all of a soporific nature. My transformation into a Communist is always associated in my memory with catnaps and a sore head.

Whenever I felt particularly sorry for myself, Karel told me, "You haven't seen anything yet. Wait till winter."

The first snow fell in October. I was still sufficiently inexperienced to regard it with pleasure, remembering how at school we had soaked our ski boots with linseed oil and waxed our skis, though we'd known that the first snowfall invariably turned into slush. How I wished I had my ski boots at Heiligendorf! Sneakers in the snow are the nearest thing to going barefoot.

At night we piled our flimsy blankets together and slept in a heap, drawing lots for who would have to sleep on the drafty outside. Only Abri continued to sleep by himself. We gave him the thickest of our collection of blankets and did not question his choice. Though we existed only as a group, there were certain exceptions which were permitted without comment. Abri's inability to endure the touch of other bodies was one of these.

Still, if I had to choose between cold and hunger, I would choose the cold. I thought we had been hungry before. But being hungry on two insufficient meals a day is not the same as being hungry on no food at all. When the snow was too deep to make the camp easily accessible, there simply was no food. There was no harm in our dying of hunger. Colonel Shit could always get a new shipment of workers for the factory. In Dachau and Buchenwald, Heiligendorf was considered a desirable place to be sent to.

There were some unexpected things I learned about hunger

that winter. That it is the most painful of diseases, for one. And that you can get high on not eating, the way you can on drugs. It really works. Whenever I read about hunger strikers now, I am suspicious of their motives. Though in my opinion the kicks aren't worth the pain.

Being high—on drugs or lack of food—makes one careless. There were constant accidents at the munitions factory. No one minded if we blew ourselves up, but the waste of ammunition was always punished, often by hanging.

The deer used to come close to the camp and gnaw the bark from the trees. There were no trees within the barbed-wire enclosure. The guards shot the deer, but of course they did not share the meat with us.

Many people died. It was not difficult. They lay down at night and were dead by morning.

Others died violently. A boy who snatched a piece of venison from one of the dogs was beaten to death by the guard to whom the dog belonged.

A man who had been a banker in private life caught sight of Colonel Shit in his garden, crumbling bread on the snow for the birds. He jumped at him and snatched the bread. One of the guards, thinking perhaps the banker had gone berserk and was attacking the camp commander, shot him down. He died, his mouth full of bread and blood. Colonel Shit bent down and carefully freed a clump of Christmas roses from the weight of the snow.

The Reds survived. Jacques and some of his friends brought us gifts of food, though they often went hungry themselves. Karel made for us a set of rules, as unbreakable as a chain.

1. Everything must be shared. If we managed to get one crumb it was imperative to divide it by six, even if the result had to be looked for with a magnifying glass.

2. No one was to do anything prejudicial to the others in order to obtain food. If we could not trust each other we would probably not survive. (This was no idle warning. The guards,

disliking any close coalition, repeatedly tried to bribe us with offers of food.)

3. Mensheviks might eat human flesh (or so rumor had it about Karel's enemy in 4C), but Bolsheviks did not. I must say that this was never one of my temptations, and I did not really believe the rumors about the Menshevik. We did eat just about everything else.

I do not know how Karel would have enforced obedience without our consent. But we all knew that Karel's chain was a life line.

We forgot by and by that the winter would ever end, that inevitably the snow would thaw and the stacked, frozen corpses would be buried. We forgot we had ever been warm, forgot even the meaning of the word. Like people lost on a polar expedition who have no choice but to eat snow and wait till they die, we went through each day with no thought of reprieve, too numb and beaten and hungry to hope. Then in February, long before the first bare patches of the meadow freed crocus and snowdrops, something better than warmth or a meal reached us—the name of a town none of us had ever heard of: Stalingrad.

It was only a name at first. A town somewhere in Russia. A name that did not appear on the German newscasts and was persistently jammed on the BBC. (Jacques and some of his friends had a radio hidden in a bucket in the stables.) It was in fact that jamming which first drew Jacques's interest to the name of Stalingrad. It was a town on the Volga, a spearhead of the German army. Outside Stalingrad people were as cold and hungry and mortal as we. These people were German soldiers, and they never entered the city.

Hindsight and history have made Stalingrad the watershed of the war. We did not see it like that at the time. We felt as a lost polar expedition might have at the sight of a plane searching for them. It might never find them. It might come too late. But there was a chance.

The warm weather held finally in April. Chilblains itched to insanity and slowly healed, the road to the camp was open once more, the frozen corpses were buried, new prisoners arrived from Dachau and Mauthausen to take their place, and everyone who had survived grew temperamental. Fights broke out, long-standing quarrels were revived, we hated each other more than we hated the guards. This was standard, I learned. Summer was tolerable and winter hell, but spring was plain nasty. Karel's rules protected us here too.

4. We love each other even when we hate each other's guts.

The Reds did not quarrel. The Reds had no fights. Dieter's smile might be more irritating than itching chilblains, Paul and Franticek so obtuse you wanted to knock their wooden heads together, I might overflow with self-pity and Karel be intolerably bossy, but we were friends, by God.

This was a necessity, for the guards did not like spring, either, and were delighted to interfere in any fight with whichever end of a rifle was more convenient. It didn't pay to have a broken head at Heiligendorf. And the tantrums passed.

My self-pity that spring took the form of deciding that if they were going to treat me like this for being a Jew I would damned well become a Jew and let them see how they liked that.

My first problem was that I did not know how one became a Jew. Except for my Catholic grandparents I had never met any Jews until Heiligendorf, and I didn't like the looks of most of the ones in camp. This was not so much anti-Semitism (I hope) as pure irritation. They reminded me of the Slavs who worked the farms at Pankow. If a cottage burned down they pulled their shawls over their heads and prayed instead of putting out the fire.

Karel maintained this attitude had nothing to do with being Jewish; it was the fault of the class system. "Lord Arsy d'Arsy here has breakfast in bed, and the poor serf whose cottage burns down probably gets whipped and put in jail."

"There hasn't been a serf in East Prussia since eighteen fifty."

"It doesn't matter what you call them. It's no good freeing serfs without giving them their own land."

"Oh, please don't tell us about Stolypin again. I couldn't stand it."

"It wouldn't do you any harm, Tyl. You still have some very bourgeois notions, you know. You have caviar and champagne for dinner, the poor serfs are lucky if they get a bone with some gristle for Christmas, and you expect the bastards to be full of spunk and come out fighting."

"They can have the caviar as far as I'm concerned. It tastes like seaweed tapioca. Anyway, what about revolutions? They're made by serfs and the poor, aren't they?"

"Revolutions are made by intellectuals," said Abri. "Though they usually allow the poor to do their fighting for them. And none of it has anything to do with the Jewish attitude Tyl was talking about, Karel. All this *oy weh ist mir* is really a form of conceit. We think it's distinguished to suffer. It shows there's something special about us."

"It shows," said Karel, "you haven't the sense to come out of the rain."

Abri seemed the obvious person to go to for information. Like Karel and the rest of the Reds he was of course an atheist. But it was not religion I wanted in any case.

I said, "Abri, how do you become a Jew?"

He gave me a startled look. "Jews are born, not made."

"But that's the problem. I was born one, at least half a one, but I wasn't made. I was raised Lutheran and the Elies were Catholics."

"That's a terribly fucked-up family, those Pankows," said Karel.

"I know. Were you raised as a proper Jew, Abri?"

"Yes. My father was a Hasid."

"What's a Hasid?"

"Now you've really asked one," said Karel. Abri just gave

me a look, the kind grownups give to children who have not yet learned not to ask a certain kind of question: how far away is the sky? who is God? where does the ebb tide go?

The face of Raphael's young cardinal against the dirty barracks wall. He said, "A Hasid must be like a child who can laugh while weeping."

"I've never seen you do either," said Karel.

"A Hasid is something you are, not something you inherit. They'd have thrown me out years ago."

"I expect they've stopped laughing by now," I said.

"Not if they are Hasidim. 'The Lord listens to those who sing in the midst of their troubles.' "

"They must be cracked."

"Surely. It's a good madness, though. I wouldn't mind having it."

"There's no such thing as a good madness," said Tyl the doctor's son.

Abri shook his head. "Give it up," he said kindly. "If you believe that you'll never make a Jew."

The arrival of the eight fliers was our first excitement in a year. They arrived at night and were locked into 4D, which was not a proper barracks but a shed at the edge of the camp which no one had used since a typhus epidemic had killed most of the prisoners who had lived there.

By morning everyone in the camp knew that (a) they were spies who had been parachuted into the mountains, (b) they were saboteurs who had come up the Danube in a new type of submarine to blow up the munitions plant, (c) they were the crew of an English bomber shot down by the Heiligendorf flak. This last, while the least fanciful, was also considered the least likely; the Heiligendorf flak had so far scored only one hit: a cow which had accidentally got into the way of a falling shell.

At the munitions plant Jacques told us that no shot-down

plane had so far been found, a piece of information which greatly strengthened the submarine-up-the-Danube faction.

That night Karel said, "Can you speak English, Abri?"

Abri said he spoke Russian, Polish, German, French, Greek, Latin, and Hebrew but no English.

Karel said crossly that he seemed to have wasted his father's hard-earned money at the university, and that surely no one in the world was plagued with such a fucked-up and useless group of comrades as he. "Tyl, what about you? Didn't they teach you English at that snob's paradise where you went to school?"

"Yes, but I think I've forgotten most of it. Why?"

"I'm going to call on the fliers."

"Call on. . . . Why all this etiquette all of a sudden? If you get caught they'll grind you up for mouse sausage, you know that."

"I won't get caught."

"But why, Karel? What's so special about the fliers?"

"They're English."

"So what?"

The abyss of ignorance revealed in my question shocked Karel into complete, if temporary, speechlessness. England, Abri mockingly informed me, was to Karel what the Holy Land was to the Crusader, the British Museum Library his Church of the Holy Sepulchre. Here Karl Marx had spent years doing research—free, mind you—for *Das Kapital*.

Karel aimed a kick at Abri, but his mind wasn't in it. He missed.

I had met only one Englishman in my life. He was called Cousin Radcliffe (one of my grandmother's foreign relations), a desiccated beanpole of a man with a long yellow mustache, long yellow teeth, and a luxuriant stammer. He descended upon East Prussia at intervals: "B-b-boar hunting, old b-boy." He was an object of fascination to my brothers and me and a source of endless hilarity to my parents and Gabriel. For years the simple repetition of "B-b-boar hunting, old b-boy" could send the entire family off into gales of laughter.

Cousin Radcliffe shared my grandfather's Communist phobia, and I could not imagine him giving free use of a reading room to Karl Marx. I told Karel as much and was sternly informed that England was fortunately not entirely inhabited by my fucked-up relations but boasted a splendidly active and strong Communist Party which had been on the verge of taking over the country when World War II had sidetracked it temporarily into fighting a more immediate enemy.

While I listened to Karel's lengthy exposition of the rise of communism in England, I tried to remember suitable phrases from my English class at St. Pölten. Welcome to Camp Heiligendorf? Well, hardly.

At midnight, when the guards changed, Karel told Jasper we were going to call on 4D. Jasper warned us not to get caught, since the fall of Naples and the Russian arrival at the Dnieper had put Colonel Shit into an exceedingly bad mood and he would with the slightest encouragement massacre the lot of us, himself—Jasper—included.

We found the RAF busily digging a tunnel under the wooden flooring. It turned out that they all spoke German well enough to spare me from having to deliver myself of my English welcome speech. None of them resembled Cousin Radcliffe, nor did they look as if they had even been on a boar hunt. (We children were always made to watch from the safety of a tree, but all the same it was wildly exciting.) Karel informed them that tunneling had been tried but that there was seepage from the river which made it all too apparent to the guards that unauthorized activities had been indulged in. Depending on the guard and Colonel Shit's mood (bad at the moment), such activities could as easily end on the meathooks as not.

A stocky, dark-haired flier, whose name was John, said it looked like the meathooks from where they sat in any case, and how long did it take?

"Twenty minutes, half an hour," Karel told him unsympathetically. I could see the tunneling had upset him. It was against all his rules for survival.

"I expect it seems longer," said a blond, untidy flier whose name was Peter.

"The thing is," said Karel, "that with Colonel Shit you don't know. He may hang you; then again he may not. He may even decide to hang only one or two of you and leave the choice up to you."

"I wonder who's the most unpopular of us," drawled Peter. He was young and quite good-looking and his teeth seemed fine, but there was something about him that was beginning to remind me of Cousin Radcliffe.

"It doesn't matter who's the most unpopular," said John. "You can't make a choice like that."

"It would be madly embarrassing," agreed Peter.

"It would be more than embarrassing," said someone from the dark. "It would be murder."

"That's Piers," said John. "*His* father's a clergyman."

Encouraged by John's tone of voice Karel asked a few questions, got the right answers, and happily discovered another comrade. Peter, too, it seemed, was one of us, but with a tarnished background, his father being a peer. Karel said generously that it was nothing, look at Tyl here, descended from the Teutonic Knights, no less, as fucked-up a background as you could hope to meet. He gave John all the cigarettes we had been hoarding, and we left. Somehow I did not feel that it had been a satisfactory visit.

Two mornings later Colonel Shit appeared during the morning newscast (Allies thrown back south of Cassino). The fliers, who had not so far joined us either in the morning or at meals, were brought out and given places with an unobstructed view of the gallows.

Colonel Shit, with that jovial reasonableness he invariably displayed at such occasions, said mildly that he could not imagine an activity more reprehensible than spying, that it was befitting neither an officer nor a gentleman, that it was indeed unspeakably revolting, but that he hoped he was neither an unjust nor an arbitrary man. His duty was plain before him, but he had never been the kind of person who is unwilling to temper justice with—not mercy, perhaps, since that was a word that did not belong in a fighting man's vocabulary, but—let us say, patience. It went against his code as an officer to hang another officer, even one belonging to an enemy nation. As he had told them repeatedly, the debt they owed the Reich for their odious activities could be repaid in other ways than with their lives. He appreciated courage but not stupid recklessness. Let it never be said that he had left a single stone unturned. One picture, he always said, was worth a thousand words. If a small demonstration would help them to reconsider, they might certainly have it. The camp was fortunate in being full of people who were entirely expendable.

His eyes went along the rows of prisoners. I never envied the people in front or at the outer edges of the barrack squares at such times; it was one of Karel's most strictly enforced rules that we were never to be first or last in any group. But in fact it did not matter. Without doubt Colonel Shit had decided long ago; when he said, "Blitzstein," I knew he had made his choice more than a year back, on our first morning here, when Blitzstein had vomited, as he vomited again now from fright, and pulled himself together and tried to run for it.

The rabbi caught him by his sleeve and held him until two guards came to collect him. He was very small and light and took a long time to die.

But it was not the pain of his slow strangling I minded. Pain is never so much of the present as of the past and the future. One suffers most in recollection and anticipation of further pain. That is why in the camp the quarry was considered a worse punishment than the gallows. But the memory of Blitzstein's thin arm, held for the guards by the one person he should have been able to trust, half murdered me, too, that half hour, though Karel stood at my shoulder and I knew that as long as he lived it could never happen to me.

Only one of the English fliers was hanged in the square. After that Colonel Shit had the gallows dug up and moved to the empty strip of meadow behind 4D, where they were out of sight of the camp but in full view—day and night—of the English fliers. I suppose Colonel Shit considered this none of the camp's business. It was between him and the fliers. Perhaps he had even grown tired of hanging us. There was so little sport to it: shooting fish in a barrel. The English fliers were a more stimulating enemy.

I am ashamed to admit that the camp agreed with Colonel Shit. We were glad his eye was off us, and the only thing that interested us was who would inherit the dead men's fleece-lined RAF boots and leather flying jackets. (How right they are now to haunt my dreams.)

Needless to say it was the guards who fell heir to boots and jackets, though Martin Lenz presently got a pair of the boots. None of us tried to take them away from him. I think there was a general feeling (certainly I felt it) that, poor boy, he'd earned them.

I don't know what the permutations of the number eight are. I'm sure Colonel Shit worked them all. And with three fliers still alive, he stopped.

The three left were John, Peter, and Piers. To this day I don't know their last names or whether they were in fact spies.

Colonel Shit stopped the hangings in November. The grapevine by way of Jasper, Martin Lenz, and Karel brought a Christmas present of reassurance to 4D. Colonel Shit had grown bored and had given up. And on Christmas morning Piers was found dead, on the electric barbed wire.

He had not died trying to escape. His hands had grasped hold of the barbed wire; even in death one could see the deliberation.

Dear Captain Aspinall, I don't know if you've ever seen

someone who's been electrocuted. I suppose it was quick, at least.

Colonel Shit would not allow John and Peter to bury the corpse. But it wasn't too bad, really. I mean, it was winter. By the time the spring thaws came, the dogs and the crows had had most of it.

This morning when I came in, I found a note pinned to my pillow. Not a lover's note, a psychologist's. "If you want to talk, please come to my room, any time at all. Don't worry about waking me."

Migaud chooses to misunderstand its intention, not surprisingly, considering what he knows of me. He says, "One day you will seduce this Captain Aspinall, and you know what these Americans are. He will feel obliged to suicide himself."

Now there's a temptation. But Migaud overestimates my capacity for boredom.

I did half consider sliding a drawing of Piers under Aspinall's door. I made one once, trying to rid myself of a ghost. But I burned it. It can't be conveyed. It can't even be experienced. One develops too many defenses, and feelings grow protected. Only the nightmares remain, the one way in which we can still experience undulled terror and grief. So let us not babble to Captain Aspinall. We owe it to our past to keep our nightmares intact.

4

July 20, 1944, was a bland and sunny day. A day without portent. Larks in the sky, Martin Lenz and I in Colonel Shit's garden, the bittersweet smell of crushed rose leaves on my scratched hands.

There were no signs in that day. No pain, no warning, no unexplained terror or joy. I tied up roses. Martin Lenz pulled weeds.

That morning Colonel Shit had told Jasper to keep back two boys to tidy up his garden. Martin Lenz was his first choice, naturally. I, for some reason, was his second.

In the open window Radio Ostmark was not unpleasantly in competition with the larks. Dishwashing music, my mother used to call it, because the maids in the kitchen used to listen to it all day long. But though I was named for Franziska's favorite piece of music I am not musical, and I found the shopworn shopgirl tunes enjoyable.

If I was not at ease it was merely because I was at all times too frightened of Colonel Shit to be relaxed so near his house. Also I would have preferred another working companion. I was shy of Lenz and what I knew about him, and could not think of anything to say to him.

The fanfare blast from the radio came so unexpectedly it made me jump. In the beginning of the war the fanfares had sounded almost daily to announce our victories: Warsaw and Paris taken, destroyers sunk, Spitfires shot down. The flourishes had diminished gradually, at first in importance, then in frequency. Until that afternoon I had not realized that we had not heard the *Sondermeldung* fanfares for many months.

Martin and I stared at each other. I could read my own thoughts in his face: Shit, we're starting to win the war again.

"Today an attempt was made on the Führer's life with explosives. The Führer suffered no injuries beyond light burns and bruises. He resumed work immediately and—as scheduled—received the Duce for lengthy discussion. Shortly after the attempt on the Führer's life he was joined by the Reichsmarshall."

The national anthem, the *Horst Wessel Lied*—I just stood there, gaping, my mouth open. Then the door crashed back and Colonel Shit stood in the garden, staring at us, his face purple. I thought he was having a heart attack. Then I saw the tears in his eyes. I couldn't believe it.

"Pankow."

"Yes, sir."

"What are you gaping at?"

"Nothing, sir."

"If you find the work here so tiring, suppose you try the quarry for a while."

"Yes, sir."

I looked to see what had happened to Martin Lenz. He, less—a million times less—stupid than I, had retreated behind a blue hedge of larkspur.

They'd heard about it at the munitions plant, of course. When I told Karel what the immediate consequence for me had been, his mouth straightened, but he had nothing to say.

At one in the morning the loud-speakers connected with the radio in Colonel Shit's house blared out the Führer's address. We'd been kept standing in the barracks square since dinnertime and were frankly glad to hear him. He referred to the attempted assassination as a crime unparalleled in German history and accepted his safety as the will of Providence. The Propaganda Minister, too, took the occasion to thank Providence for the protection of the Führer. And then at last we were allowed to go to sleep.

There are three infallible ways of driving people mad: drugs, complete isolation, and backbreaking work without object or reward or end.

This was the purpose of the quarry. It was completely worked out and used only for punishment. The prisoners broke up worthless rock, carted it from one end to the other and back again. They were encouraged to look busy by a guard with a carbine.

A few prisoners had gone mad in the quarry. One had killed himself by beating his brains out against the rock. Others had been murdered by their fellow prisoners. Others had survived. One could see them about the camp with faces like an empty wall.

The first day wasn't bad. It rained, for one thing, which settled the dust. And I didn't yet mind breaking rock.

In a place like Heiligendorf, where all enmity, bad temper, and misery must remain unexpressed, one can build up a formidable amount of hostility. At the end of that first day my hands were bleeding, but I looked with satisfaction at a pile of broken enemies at my feet.

Karel met me with a mug of water. "It wasn't so bad," I told him.

"Wait and see," he said.

The next day the sun shone. My shoulders and back were so sore I could barely move them. My hands were covered with broken and inflamed blisters.

"Enjoy yourself," said Karel.

It is not possible to remember physical pain exactly. I have only a dazed kind of memory of that day and the ones that followed.

"Wait till you stop hurting," said Karel. "That's when it gets really bad." He knew about the quarry. He'd spent four weeks in it once. He never told me why.

I ached for about a week. Then my hands calloused, my back grew used to the work, and the only physical pains I was left with were hunger and thirst.

Karel was right. Pain, like love, makes the time pass. It is a source of self-absorption, an occupation; it was a protection against the realization that all of it, hunger and thirst and back-breaking labor, was for nothing. We broke rock and carted it from one side of the quarry to the other and back again.

Every day the sun burnt down from a cobalt sky. Stone dust hung in the air, lay on my tongue, gritted between my teeth. In one way I was lucky: I tan quickly. Some of the others were so sunburned their skin hung from them in swatches. At the edge of the quarry, black boots and a carbine were outlined against the cloudless sky.

The guard's name was Gustav Klug. The Americans have him now and will put him on trial and I will not give evidence, as I have not given evidence against any of the others. But if Gustav Klug is as clever as his name, he is spending his days praying for a long prison sentence.

After a while I stopped feeling hungry. For the first time since I arrived at Heiligendorf I did not crave food. I ate stone dust all day and it fed me. Karel bullied me into swallowing the boiled vomit, the mouse sausage, the moldy bread. I was too apathetic to fight him. Had I done so, I am certain he would have fed me by holding my mouth and nose closed till I had to swallow. It is the way one force-feeds the insane.

All day there was thirst. It never left me. Even while I was drinking water I was thirsty. Karel met me with a bucketful every evening. I drank it all, throwing up and drinking more. I never had enough. I could have lived on it.

At night Karel climbed into my bunk, bringing me bits of food Jacques had given him: windfall apples, a piece of cheese sometimes, and once, unbelievably, a square of chocolate. I swallowed it because Karel stuck it in my mouth. It didn't oc-cur to me till long after that it had not been shared six ways, that the apples, the cheese, the occasional end of a loaf of good bread from the farm were all given to me to be ungratefully swallowed as if they were medicine.

I was afraid of falling asleep, for in my dreams I broke rock and ate dust. It was Karel who held me, night after night, who said, "I know, Tyl, I know; I was down there for four weeks once and crazy for another four after that; it doesn't matter, the only thing that matters is to survive; go to sleep, Tyl, I'll stay with you." It was Karel too who gave me the final brutal shove every morning when I was certain I could not face it another day. "Get going, Tyl. Shit's just waiting for you to get temperamental. Don't do him any favors. It can't last forever."

I was not concerned with forever. This was the day I could not bear.

"Get going, you lazy bastard. You're not at Pankow now. This is how the other side lives. Do you good to find out. Get with it."

And another sun-scorched, dust-choked day.

That summer: 1944, tourist weather, flier weather, weather for boating and swimming and mountain climbing. Austria, that green, rain-soaked country, for once had a dry summer.

It was the torturer's summer, too, and the hangman's; a summer for wholesale arrests of anyone even remotely suspected of being connected with the July twentieth plot. While I ate stone dust, German generals were tortured in the cellars of the Gestapo prison in Berlin, were hanged as slowly and painfully as any prisoner at Heiligendorf. I do not know by what grapevine Jacques got this news. All I know is that by subsequent reports they were proved correct, and that I, whom these remote events were soon to touch and transform into traitor, murderer, whore, and lover, paid no attention to them whatever.

There were seven of us in the quarry that summer. I knew only two by name: a man called Uspenski from 4B and a boy—Tovah something or other—from our barracks. We never spoke. It wasn't allowed, but even if the guard had permitted it I doubt whether we would have. To get through the day was all that counted. We had no interest to waste on anything else.

Uspenski had been down the longest. He was a Communist, an old enemy of Karel's, one of the Menshevik's adjutants, as wild and furious as his master. He was in fine shape. Hatred kept him going. He hated the guards, Colonel Shit, and Jews. It sustained him through each day.

Tovah had nothing. The rabbi never bothered to look after any of his people who were in trouble. No one met him when he dragged himself out of the quarry at night; there was no one to bring him water or make him eat. Every evening he lay by the water tap until someone pushed him aside. Because he was the least defended of us the guard picked on him the most, and when the guard wasn't hounding him Uspenski took over. And so it was Tovah, not I, who one morning sat down on the rock and refused to go on. I think the guard was glad of it. It was a boring job for him just to stand and watch us.

He shouted down, "I'll have to shoot the lazy bastard if he doesn't get up. Of course the bullets'll ricochet if I happen to miss, and you might all get hurt. You, Uspenski, why don't you use your pickax and take care of it for me?"

Uspenski was a swine, but no Communist ever did anything to help a Nazi guard. "Go fuck your carbine," he muttered. "Get up, you miserable shit!" he then roared at Tovah, who sat and looked at him without any sign of response on his face.

"All right, stand aside and hope for the best," Klug shouted. "I've got my orders, you know. Stand aside now, quick!"

But the others, not Uspenski, closed in on Tovah, who made no move to defend himself. Klug did nothing. He'd known this would happen. It always did.

It was very quick. There wasn't anything Uspenski or I could do in time. By the time we broke through their circle there was no longer any point to it. It was kinder to the boy to let them finish.

When Karel brought me my water that night, he said, "That does it. You're coming out of there, Tyl."

I said, "How nice," never thinking he could do it. But he did.

I realized afterwards that he must have been working on his plan for weeks. Tovah's death merely made the final decision for him.

I can't even make a suspense story of it, which is a pity, for it was a neatly contrived murder. But the truth is that I lived too deeply in a dark, small hole in my mind, full of stone dust and jagged, broken rocks, to feel interest, far less suspense. I did not even resent Karel's absence the next few nights. He was gone, that was all, talking for hours to Jasper, moving through the dark intervals of the searchlights to 4D to visit the fliers.

Afterwards it was simple to fit together the pieces. Colonel Shit was not a suicidal type, and, whatever the note left behind claimed, he most certainly was not one of the July twentieth conspirators.

A combination of circumstances made the murder not only possible but reasonably safe. Karel wanted me out of the quarry and as usual took the most direct route to achieve his way. The RAF fliers had cyanide and Jasper had access to Colonel Shit's food. Whether it was true that in the aftermath of the assassination attempt Colonel Shit had once more begun to eye the surviving English fliers with displeasure, had discovered Jasper's sexual tastes and was planning to cure them on the Russian front, or whether Karel merely invented these stories to get their cooperation for his plan, I have never found out. I do know that he had learned from Jasper that no army officer's reputation was safe, and that no official investigation would follow a confessed "July twentieth" suicide.

And so Colonel Shit was found dead one morning by his orderly, the confession neatly by his side. No investigation followed. Colonel Shit was buried without honors. The sun continued to shine, and the work in the quarry went on.

5

For two weeks the camp was run by the most senior of the guards, Sergeant Steiger, who was far too respectful of the late camp commander's institutions to make any changes. Then a new camp commander arrived (in a Mercedes, rumor had it, but driving himself, which was a nice change from Colonel Shit, who couldn't go to the lavatory without an armed guard). I was down in the quarry and did not see him until, on his survey of his new command, he came to the edge of the rocks. I looked up to see fine boots, the black triangle of an arm carried in a sling, a black eye patch, the black uniform, hatefully familiar.

Familiar, I saw suddenly, but not hateful. The uniform was black, but the emblems and crimson piping on the collar were those of the Panzer corps, not the SS.

The relief was so great it made my knees buckle. I did not stop to question what qualifications had turned a tank corps officer into Colonel Shit's successor. The reassurance was as great as it was irrational; this was Gabriel's uniform: the envy, admiration, and ambition of my childhood.

Sergeant Steiger was explaining the purpose of the quarry to him, pointing at us. I bent to my work again. It didn't pay to be seen watching.

The explosion followed the explanation without pause. SS or tank corps, he had a temper. It was, however, for once not directed at us.

"Out!" he ordered. "All of you. Get out at once. Drop those pickaxes—"

"But *Herr General*—"

"Silence! Come out. No one is ever to be made to work there again. Is that understood?"

The senior guard clicked his heels. "Yes, *Herr General*. But may I respectfully point out—"

"You may not. Now"—he looked at us, a skeptical group, covered with quarry dust—"how will we ever get you clean?" His one eye, very light, very blue, went to the river that tantalized us beyond the barbed wire every summer. "Good," he said. "Have a swim. Off you go."

"But, sir, the barbed wire is electrified," said Steiger.

"Well, turn the electricity off. And don't turn it on again."

"But, *Herr General*—"

The pale eye turned from the river to the guard's face and rested there. "Yes?"

"Nothing, sir. At your orders."

The river was cold, fed by the melted mountain snows. At once our mood changed from the depression of the quarry to manic laughter. All the fortunes I've ever had told predict death by water; my fantasies of dying are always of drowning. I wondered, lying back and letting the water run into my mouth, my ears, my open eyes, whether I could not just drift off, into the Danube, clean and cold, picked to the white bone by hungry fish, till I was carried home to the sea. But our river scarcely deserved the name. At its deepest it was no more than two feet, and of course there was the guard with the carbine.

When he motioned us out our manic mood lasted up the hill. I had washed out my filthy uniform and put it on without bothering to wring it out. After the sun and dust of the quarry it was wonderful to be wet and cold.

The new camp commander stood watching us, half smiling. The emblems on his collar caught the sun. He wore no medals, but this did not give the impression that he had none. A deep scar ran down the left side of his face, cutting through the eyebrow, under the eye patch, and down the cheek and jaw. It looked recent and raw and probably hurt like hell. For all the silver and gold braid on his shoulders he was a young man, also an inhumanly tired one. Under the peaked cap a lank, light strand of hair had slid over the scarred forehead. I had at first thought that it was the same tow color as mine. Now I saw that it was white.

As I passed him he looked down at me and his face went the color of bad milk. I thought I probably looked pretty awful, but no worse than the others, surely. Not bad enough to make anyone sick.

He swallowed. "What is your name?"

"Pankow, sir."

He reached out and turned me to face him. "Yes," he said, "you have the Pankow face. Why are you here?"

"My mother is a Jew."

"Of course, you are Tyl. The doctor's son. Gabriel was your uncle. He was a very good friend of mine."

The past tense wormed its way into my mind. I loved Gabriel best of all my relatives and envied him the most, but since Heiligendorf, though I had never heard from him, he had become something more to me; my link with Outside.

"Was?"

"I am sorry. Of course you don't know. Gabriel is dead. He was killed in Africa."

I refused to take it in. "Are you sure, sir?"

The deep scar tissue, the eye patch, the scar-quirked corner of his mouth made of the left side of his face an unrevealing mask, which he kept turned to me. He said, "I am sure. I was his battalion commander. He was killed on June twenty-second, nineteen forty-two, at the end of the second battle of Tobruk." He looked down at me with sympathy and—incredibly, this was the camp commander!—with kindness and said formally, "I am sorry we must begin our acquaintance with bad news, Tyl."

It is easy afterwards to recollect too much. It has taken a conscious effort to remember that this was all: a drenched prisoner and a young, white-haired general talking in the sun, the first exchange between us the news of Gabriel's death.

When the truck pulled in and Karel saw me, he said, "You're out, Tyl. It's the fucking best news in years."

I did not tell him about Gabriel, for to Karel the only good German was a dead German, and I did not want him to say something I would find it impossible to forgive.

I said, "We're all out. Thanks, Karel."

"Nothing to do with me."

"Of course not. Thanks anyway."

"Shut up, shut up. Don't even think it. I was in bed with you that night, remember? That's all you know. You start playing guessing games and I'll kill *you*."

"All right, Karel. I think things are going to be different here from now on."

"How so?"

"This new general seems to be a good sort."

"Oh, fuck off," Karel said disgustedly. "Use your head, Tyl. Where would you get a decent German officer from?"

"No, really—"

"I think your brains shrank in the quarry. He's a general in the German army. What do you think he did to get there? Wave his wings and make like an angel?"

"Compared to Colonel Shit he probably did."

"Tyl, remember the hangings, the fliers, the Blitzstein boy, the quarry. There are no comparisons. They're all in the same business. What one does, all do."

"I suppose so."

"You know so."

After dinner the new camp commander introduced himself. He said, "I am General von Svestrom. The electricity in the barbed-wire fence has been shut off. If any of you care to try to escape you are free to do so. I have unfortunately no control over what happens if you are picked up outside. Who runs Four A?"

No one answered.

"Don't tell me each barracks hasn't got someone in charge. Who is in charge of Four A?"

All six of us stepped forward. One couldn't be sure if he was smiling or if it was just the slant of his scarred face.

"Who is in charge of you six?"

"I guess I am," said Karel.

"What is your name?"

"Killian."

"Sir."

I could tell from the set of Karel's mouth that it was half killing him. But survivors cannot afford to make a fuss over small things. Karel said obediently, "Killian, sir."

"Why has Four A proper latrine trenches and the others not?"

Karel said, "There was typhus here when I first came. I'm scared of it," and added, "sir," as an afterthought.

"Very sensible. The other barracks will please imitate the arrangements of Four A. Killian, I want you to stay home from the munitions plant until the work is finished, and see to it that it is done properly. I intend to run a camp, not a dungheap." With which he dismissed us.

"Crusty Prussian bastard," growled Karel.

"Hell, Karel, he's a general. If you were in the army you'd have to address him properly, so why not here? And he's right about the latrines. You've been bitching about them for years."

"Oh, fuck off. You and your General Saint Svestrom."

It was like a holiday the next morning to pile into the truck for the munitions plant with the others. As we pulled out the gate, a guard came running from the camp commander's house and stopped the truck.

"Pankow, the general wants to see you, on the double."

Franticek said, "Shit, he's decimating us."

"On the double," the guard repeated.

"All right, I'm coming."

I was not frightened, only dispirited. I had lost the prisoner's most treasured asset: anonymity. Karel, who was enjoying himself supervising the Menshevik shoveling shit, gave me a worried grin and his bugger-you sign.

The camp commander was drinking coffee and smoking a cigarette. His coffee didn't smell any better than the stuff we had. This morning his arm was not in a sling. His hand was in the pocket of his black tunic, and it was difficult to tell under the sleeve just what was wrong with it. It had the twisted, lame look of a bad break, badly healed.

"Good morning, Tyl von Pankow."

"Good morning, sir."

"Can you do housework?"

"I don't know. I can try."

"Good. Then as a pure case of nepotism, because you are your uncle Gabriel's nephew, you can look after the house for me. Agreed?"

"Yes, sir. Thank you."

It was the cushiest job in camp. Colonel Shit had used it to play favors, giving it to informers in return for tales that should never have left the barracks. The only member of 4A who had ever held it had stumbled accidentally into the electric barbed-wire fence the first day on the job. Karel was standing next to him when it happened, but so were some other people.

General von Svestrom smiled. "It's a sinecure, you know. I am paranoiacally neat. Well, good-by, Tyl." At the door he stopped "By the way, if those pink geraniums in the window boxes should die of neglect, I should be quite ready to forgive you. I don't like geraniums."

I had planted those geraniums on July 20. I did not like them either.

"Yes, sir."

He left, and a moment later I saw the black Mercedes with the swastika on the door drive out the camp gates. I wondered how he managed the driving with a lame arm.

The job was a sinecure indeed. My one problem, I saw at once, would be to find enough to do, so that I could look busy if a guard passed the windows. I washed the cup and saucer (it was camp coffee) and wiped some nonexistent dust. When I was unobserved I explored.

He had unpacked, but the small house was still as anonymous as a suicide's hotel room. His uniforms were hung away in a closet, together with a navy wool shirt and gray flannels, and in the furthest corner of the closet the brown tunic of the Afrika Korps with a captain's badges on the shoulders. A cupboard held a lot of bottles, brandy mostly. Most of the drawers were empty. I even checked under the paper lining, for there was to me something suspicious in this lack of possessions. But I found nothing. No letters, no photographs.

In one drawer were his medals. As I had suspected, he had the lot, including the *Ritterkreuz* with oak leaves. With the medals was another thing he didn't wear: a seal ring. Perhaps he considered it too elaborate to wear. It looked old and valuable, something belonging in a museum: a large, flawed lapis lazuli, a lady with a unicorn in her lap cut to hide the flaw, the inscription "*A mon seul désir*" carved in the stone.

By the bed was a small pile of books. I turned them in my hand, forgetting even my curiosity for a moment in the pleasure of turning a page; I had not held a book in my hands for two years. When I looked down I saw it was in French. *Le côté de Guermantes.* I wasn't sure how well I could still read French; I hadn't tried since school. But it looked as if I would have the leisure to find out. Two of the books were in German. One was an Insel paperback called *The Life and Death of Cornet*

Christopher Rilke; the other, *Death in Venice,* had been Gabriel's favorite. I could still remember his rage when the Propaganda Ministry had banned it. Open, face down on the floor, was a book in English called *The Picture of Dorian Gray*. I could only make out a word here and there. I had forgotten most of the English they had taught us at school.

The flyleaf of each book except the *Dorian Gray* was signed Johannes v. Svestrom. *Dorian Gray* had a purple stamp across each page: Mercy Hospital, Rastenburg.

The bathroom contained the usual things: comb, brush, razor, soap (nice soap, French), toothpaste, and two toothbrushes, almost new, with thick, stiff bristles. I was tempted to use one, my own having achieved the texture of a fine sable watercolor brush over the last two years. But at the idea of borrowing a major general's toothbrush, my gall failed me. I did squeeze some toothpaste on my finger and cleaned my teeth that way. It tasted marvelous.

The medicine cupboard was locked and I could not get it open without breaking the lock. On the door of the medicine cabinet was a mirror. I looked at my face in it for a long time. It was the first time I had seen myself in two years.

During my time in the quarry I had let my hair grow as protection from the sun. Streaks of it were bleached almost white. I was very thin, of course, but I was in terrific shape from the quarry and I had a wonderful tan. My nose was peeling and freckled, my mouth raw. I seemed to have developed in those two years a formidable scowl. To be frank, I was pleased with myself. But I could not imagine how General von Svestrom had seen any resemblance to the handsome, debonair Gabriel.

Strange that Gabriel, dead two years, should still be doing me kindnesses.

In the afternoon I dug up the pink geraniums and carried them to 4C, where the Menshevik was at long last, under Karel's ferocious supervision, coming to grips with the sanitation problem. I threw the geraniums on top of the mess. "Flowers from Colonel Shit. Sweets to the sweet."

The Menshevik growled but said nothing. I was not at that moment a safe person to offend. Karel and I stood at a safe distance upwind and talked for a moment, but a guard had his eye on us, so I went back to the camp commander's house and read *Cornet Christopher Rilke*. Rilke was, like me, a graduate of St. Pölten, though neither he nor the school had a high opinion of each other. When the munitions works trucks pulled in the gate, I set General von Svestrom's table for dinner and went back to the barracks.

One of the bastard guards was on after dinner, so we kept quiet. At midnight Jasper took over, and in a moment all the Reds were crowded in my bunk.

"Did you snoop around?"

"Sure. There's nothing. He's got a locked medicine cabinet, but I couldn't get in without leaving a mark. Nothing else at all."

"No food neither?"

"Not a fucking crumb."

"If there is you leave it alone," said Karel. "He catches you pinching food, he might just put you on latrine duty at Four C. You keep your nose clean, Tyl."

"Is he a queer?"

"Huh?"

"A queer. A faggot, a fairy, a homosexual—you know. Likes boys?"

"I really don't know," I said, finding myself resenting these remarks on General von Svestrom's behalf. "What makes you ask?"

"It's always the first thing you try to find out."

"Must be something," said Franticek. "Nobody keeps that clean without something to hide."

"Does he have any books?" asked Abri.

"Four."

"What are they?" Karel asked.

"*The Communist Manifesto, The ABC of Communism, Das Kapital,* and *Little Red Riding Hood in the Kremlin.*"

Karel pulled my hair, hard.

"*Death in Venice,* by Thomas Mann—"

"That's a queer book," said Abri, our intellectual.

"—Rilke, a French one called *Le côté de Guermantes,* and one in English by someone called Oscar Wilde. *The Picture of Dorian Gray,* it's called."

"They're all queer books," said our intellectual.

"The Rilke isn't. I read it this afternoon."

"He's got to be a queer," said Karel.

"Nobody but a queer would read novels," said Franticek.

"Well, I'm going to read them, except the *Dorian Gray* one. I like novels."

"All the better," said Franticek.

"What do you mean, all the better?"

"Logic," said Abri. "If you read novels you're a fairy and will enjoy sleeping with the general, should he be a fairy, which we certainly all hope for."

"Christ, don't you start now, Abri. What's the matter with all of you tonight?"

"Wishful thinking," said Karel. "Happy days are here again, tra la. See, Tyl, if the camp commander is poofed, the guards tend to be too, and the more buggering there is the worse camp discipline gets and the more chances for blackmail there are. The more we blackmail, the easier life is for us. Though queer or not, something about this Svestrom tells me that blackmail wouldn't cut much ice with him. So your job is really to keep him in a cheerful frame of mind."

"How?"

"By doing what he wants. Cheerfully."

"Even if it's painful," said Franticek.

"Embarrassing," said Paul.

"Humiliating," said Karel.

"Grotesque," said Abri.

I was as close to losing my temper as I ever came with Karel. All of it seemed to me both hateful and unnecessary.

"What is this, some music hall turn you worked up in Dachau? The Poof Quartet."

"Tyl," said Abri, "it's the reason we are no longer in Dachau. And that's not a joke. See, in Dachau a lot of the guards fucked around with the boys, and when Heiligendorf was opened the guards who were transferred here naturally took their favorite boys along. Unfortunately for them Colonel Shit was a maniac on the subject and packed them all off to the Russian front."

"What about Jasper?"

"Jasper's exceptional. He doesn't fuck around, for one thing, he's just got the one person, and he's discreet about it, so he wasn't suspected. Stop being so sorry for yourself, Tyl. At least you have a chance to read books again. For that I'd go to bed with Goebbels himself."

"Would you?" I said, surprised. Abri, who could not bear to be touched even by his friends, even for warmth on the coldest winter nights.

"Yes. I would."

"I'll give Svestrom your message. Better you than me any day."

"Not funny, Tyl," said Karel.

"I wasn't being funny. I meant it. I really don't think I'd like it."

Karel sat up and cracked his shaved head on a beam. "You fucking spoiled brat! Aren't you ever going to learn anything? You're not Lord Arsy d'Arsy of East Prussia now, remember. It's you he picked, not Abri. Now listen and don't forget it again. I get kind of tired of all this elementary school stuff. Anything that helps us survive is good for us. Not fun for you. Good for us, the group. Just be clear about that, Tyl. You still have a head full of bourgeois ideas."

This insult usually preceded Karel's lectures on politics. It

63

was in a way a relief to have him switch to sex, which is a more interesting subject, though Karel's paragraph-one-subsection-a approach could take a lot of the ginger out of sex too. This, however, turned out to be instruction in survival (using sex) and was worth listening to, for Karel was an experienced survivor.

Paragraph 1: The idea of the body as private property surrendered at one's will as an act of love was romantic rubbish fit at best for bourgeois reactionaries Outside.

Subsection a: For prisoners the body was a permanent liability subject to hunger, cold, pain, and the ultimate treachery, illness.

Subsection b: If by the chance of someone in power requiring this body for his fun it could be turned into an asset, it was not for us to have private sentiments.

Subsection c: All the rest was a technicality.

I could not help wishing that Karel would not be so contemptuous of technicalities. I would have liked him to go into detail, even with paragraph two, subsection a, if necessary. Karel had no idea how ignorant a cat's-paw he was sending out.

He gave me a puff of his cigarette and said, "That's understood, then."

I said, "Yes, Karel," for it would have been hard to fault the logic of his exposition.

He swung down from my bunk to his own. The others followed him, leaving me alone, open-eyed in the dark. My thoughts went back to the camp commander's house. What secret did the lack of possessions conceal?

Perhaps there was no secret. No attempt at concealment. Only a lack of interest so great it made possessions superfluous.

And yet, even we, dispossessed as we were, had our private hoards: playing cards, a cigarette or two, a stolen bayonet, my treasured toothbrush. During the last year we had even owned a cat, a wild, half-starved battle-ax of a stray, who had walked in on us one day, had been kicked out, had come back. There was little enough garbage at Heiligendorf. We ate everything that was even dubiously edible. But we began saving and scrounging scraps for him. Karel had protested against such sentimentality, but Abri had pointed out that if worst came to worst we could always eat the cat.

Besides, he had a red coat and was obviously in the right camp politically. We named him Lenin to please Karel, till the day when Lenin, in spite of the skimpy food, swelled and proved to be pregnant. The day she gave birth to six kittens we renamed her Rosa Luxemburg. But the kittens had to go. They were too hungry.

For anyone wishing to make the experiment, there is practically no meat on a kitten and the broth tastes awful.

Rosa bore us no ill will but remained with us, warming our toes in winter and hunting field mice and meadowlarks in the summer. The rabbi hated her. He said she was dirty. Which was another reason for keeping her.

The next morning when I arrived at the camp commander's house, the senior guard was just leaving. General von Svestrom shut the door behind him and smiled at me. "He says you are dangerous. He came to warn me about you. Are you?"

I spread my hands to show how dangerous I was. I didn't even have fingernails. I used to bite them.

"Why is he afraid of you?"

"He isn't. He just wants the job for one of his own people."

"Oh, why?"

"Information, of course."

General von Svestrom laughed. "He would be very bored."

"Yes, sir."

He gave me a pale, slanting look, meaning he knew I had been snooping and didn't give a damn. It was not a comfortable look.

For something to say, I asked, "Do you want me to do anything about the garden, sir?"

He looked at the empty window boxes and Colonel Shit's well-tended garden, where late asters, roses, and clumps of chrysanthemum still bloomed. He shrugged. "There's no point in doing anything now. If we're still here in the spring we might dig up all this rubbish and put in vegetables. But the war will be over by then, I imagine. It's quite all right, Tyl, you may look pleased. I won't cut your head off for it."

"We haven't had news in months here."

"Of course. I keep forgetting how cut off you are. Please listen to the radio if you like."

"Thank you, sir."

"Well, good-by, Tyl."

I watched him get into the Mercedes and pull out of the camp gates. I wondered where he went every day. After Karel's talk I half hoped that he had perhaps a mistress in Linz whom he visited. But somehow it did not ring true. I think I had a conventional notion that mistresses only function at night.

(The truth, which was not secret, was less romantic. He did go to Linz, but only to raise hell with the local authorities and the military garrison about the conditions in camp. When that got him nowhere he began to deal directly with the local farmers for food for us. He was not very successful, for money was no longer worth much and there was nothing to barter. I think he must have employed a certain amount of blackmail, hints that the allied armies approaching so rapidly would not look kindly on farmers who had let the inmates of the camp starve, for he did manage to scrounge a truckload of turnips here, some windfall apples there, potatoes, sometimes, and cabbages that weren't quite good enough for market. In the last year of the war, that meant they were rotten. But we were grateful for anything. It was food. The mouse sausage persisted to our last day in camp, but after one look at the boiled vomit General von Svestrom informed the camp cook that he would boil him in it if it were ever served again. Which made a nice change from Colonel

Shit, who had no doubt never even seen the meals we were served, let alone eaten them.)

The bathroom cabinet was still locked. I looked at the books again. In spite of Abri's sinister interpretation, they seemed to me simply the first handful a person might take from his shelf when he went on a trip. Gabriel or my father would have come up with the same unrelated selection.

I could still make nothing of *Dorian Gray,* but my French was good enough for Proust. I dived into it headlong and didn't come up for air until dark.

Beginning *A la recherche du temps perdu* in the middle is confusing, but I've read it straight through since (it was the first book I stole when I got to Vienna) and I suspect it doesn't make too much difference where one starts it. *Le côté de Guermantes* may even be a good beginning; it is much the most entertaining of all the books, though *Albertine Disparue* is now my favorite.

Svestrom's copy was only part two of *Guermantes,* ending with the scene where Monsieur Charlus snubs Bloch at the theater. Why did I love it so much? It was an unlikely book for a boy in a prison camp to enjoy. Perhaps it was its very unlikeliness that pleased me. Nothing could have been farther from Heiligendorf than Proust's Paris. Yet these people were familiar. The Guermantes' stupidity would have transplanted well to East Prussia. My grandfather and his neighbors lacked the Guermantes' glamor, but they were certainly their equals in snobbery.

In the evening I remembered General von Svestrom's permission to listen to his radio. The dial was set to the shortwave BBC station. This was a fantastic piece of carelessness. People did of course listen to the BBC. At least Monsignor Hesbach always had. It was probably the most widely broken law in Germany. But it was a capital offense, and I would have felt more reassured about Svestrom if he had made a concession to the danger by switching back to the *Deutschlandsender.* I did it for him.

It was not easy to make much of the news reports, which

were filled with the evasions of defeat: strategic withdrawals, consolidations of the line, insignificant break-throughs. But the place names told much. Aachen, the Moselle, the Vistula. Our borders were drawing in upon Germany once more. The Russians were in East Prussia. I wished them well.

Perhaps they would use Pankow to quarter their troops. It is a big house. They would be comfortable. They could tear up the parquet for firewood and use the green and gold Meissen dinner service for target practice. There was a convenient lantern in front of the stables from which they could hang the Rittmeister.

Pankow—the eye made free of the flat brown land with the gray swath of the Baltic at its edge. The small forest of ship's masts in the carpenter's yard, gulls squatting like pigeons in the kitchen garden, turf fires and the smell of wild thyme, the touch of my mother's Judas kiss on my cheek.

Take it and welcome!

After dinner Karel said, "Did he?"

"Sure. Long distance. Didn't you see the car has been gone all day?"

"Where does he go, do you know?"

"Mhm. He has a mistress in Linz."

"Damn," said Karel. "That's too bad."

Not satisfied with improving the camp food, the mistress in Linz next came across with a truckload of new uniforms. Not the striped prison uniforms, but denim Luftwaffe fatigues.

"A flier friend of mine in Vienna got a shipment by mistake," Svestrom explained. "I thought we needed them more than he, so I talked him out of them. Will you see to it that they're distributed without too much of a scramble, Tyl? What's the matter?"

"Nothing, sir. They look very glamorous."

I did not expect him to understand how I felt. It is prison

clothes, not barbed wire and guards with killer dogs, which are the direct and personal symbol of captivity. There is no vanity in this, only the simple fact that clothes are nearest to the skin.

"I know," said Svestrom. "Stone walls may not a prison make, but I suspect striped uniforms most definitely make a prisoner."

"Yes. I thought one had to wear one to understand that."

"I do wear one. All uniforms imprison in some way. I suggest you burn the old ones. I don't want to see them again. Tell the guards I said to let you have a fire."

We had our bonfire and a noisy celebration around it which made the guards extremely nervous. They paced around the fire with their dogs and gave us nasty looks, but there was nothing else they could do.

It came to me suddenly that I had not thanked Svestrom. But if he was watching the bonfire, he'd probably got the message.

Karel pointed out to me that the new uniforms had four pockets, which would be a help with Operation Fuck-up. I sincerely hoped Svestrom would never find out that his good deed was about to be converted to sabotage.

The next morning I stopped by the camp barber and had my head shaved. This was not so much Nazi chicanery as a precaution against lice. Karel wasn't the only one scared of typhus.

The Menshevik in 4C and some of the religious Jews wore long hair and beards. The Menshevik maintained that he had had typhus in Siberia and one could only get it once, which is a fallacy. The Jews said God did not approve of cut hair, which sounds like a fallacy too. Most of us didn't take chances.

The weather had changed overnight. Icy rain slashed at me as I made my way to the camp commander's house. Last night's joyful bonfire was a black, sodden mess.

Svestrom had already gone. I pulled his blanket around me and settled down to read *Death in Venice*. It bored me terribly.

I was about to go back to the Guermantes when Aschenbach met the beautiful Tadzio. I decided to stick with it and try to get some information. But Thomas Mann was much too literary to deal in technicalities. I couldn't imagine what Gabriel had seen in the story.

I see now of course that I was unfair to it, perhaps because I expected something different. I've read *Death in Venice* many times since then, and I admit now that it is a masterpiece, but a masterpiece so carefully designed to fit its frame that its very perfection keeps me off. It compels my admiration, but I don't get tangled up in its guts the way I do with Proust.

I never got to finish it that day because General von Svestrom walked in on me. I'd forgotten to keep an eye on the window and an ear out for the muffler of the Mercedes, which was in bad shape.

I half jumped out of my skin. Sitting on the camp commander's bed, wrapped in the camp commander's blanket, reading the camp commander's book—hell, Colonel Shit would have had me on a meathook for any one of those things, and my instincts were trained to respond to him.

Svestrom smiled and said, "I'm sorry, Tyl, I didn't mean to make you jump." He bent to see what I was reading. "That was Gabriel's favorite story. Do you like it?"

"Not very much. I like *Le côté de Guermantes*, though."

"So you damned well should. Your accent is good. How is that?"

"My grandmother was part French. She was called Gabrielle. Gabriel was named after her. And there are French workers at the munitions plant."

His coat was dripping on the floor. I helped him off with it, careful not to hurt his bad arm. He poured himself a glass of brandy and drank it straight down.

"Do you want some, Tyl?"

"No, thank you, sir. I don't like the taste. Shall I fetch you some lunch?"

"No, don't bother. I'll have this instead."

He poured himself another glass of brandy and sat down on the bed again.

"I've been scrounging up some more food. Not much. God, how I loathe peasants." He looked tired and in pain. "Who was it said, 'The idiocy of rural life'?"

"Karl Marx."

"Dear me. Anyway, idiocy or not, I managed to get some apples and potatoes."

"You're becoming very popular."

"Just for that?"

"It's a lot to us."

He said, "I try to remember how it was at school, how hungry we always were, and of course we were fed much better than this. All the same we were forever writing home for food packages like the deserving poor. Did you go to school in Königsberg?"

"No. I was at St. Pölten."

"Why is that?"

"My mother's family all went there, and my grandparents wanted me to."

"I see. Did you like it?"

"After the first year it was all right."

"What happened the first year?"

"They'd never seen a Prussian before."

"Lord, yes. Wrong accent. When did this catch up with you?"

"The camp? Forty-two."

"Two years. It must seem forever."

I realized suddenly that for two years I had not talked with anyone like this: idly, without effort, knowing that no surprises lurked—as they always did with Karel—speaking with the same accent. It might have been Gabriel or one of my brothers. But it was the camp commander and the sooner I remembered it the better. It was too easy. It compelled my trust on no evidence. What did I know about him? That he commanded a concentration camp. That he owned four books and a drawer full of medals. That the name that stood on the flyleaf of his books in a handwriting of sharp downstrokes and secretive, narrow n's and m's—Johannes v. Svestrom—could as well stand at the foot of an order of transfer to Auschwitz or execution. And if he never made use of this power he was still its representative and I had no business feeling at home with it.

"Would you like a cigarette, Tyl?"

"Thank you, sir. Would it be all right if I didn't smoke it now? We make it a point to share everything."

"The Heiligendorf Reds?"

"That's right."

"One cigarette doesn't go very far between six people. You'd better have the pack."

Damn you, you're too good to be true. "Thank you, sir."

"What the devil have you done to your hair, Tyl?"

"Shaved it off."

"Let it grow again."

"It's safer not to. We get lousy."

He laughed. "Your uncle Gabriel and his entire company shaved their heads once, in Africa, because of some silly bet Gabriel lost. Rommel was furious."

"I should think Gabriel's company would have been the ones to be furious."

"My dear Tyl, if Gabriel had decided to cut off his nose and paint himself green, they would all have cheerfully followed suit. They worshiped him. But Rommel said he objected to one of his companies looking as if they had just completed a mass escape from a lunatic asylum. After that Gabriel always claimed that the only qualification for the Afrika Korps was a full head of hair. As a matter of fact the shaven head rather suited him. It suits you too."

I said, "Thank you," feeling silly.

He put out his hand in a half-joking gesture, and I swear I hadn't meant to do it—I'd promised Karel, for one thing, and for another, what good would it do?—but I flinched away. He put his hand back on his knee, his laughter gone, replaced not by anger but by something else which I could not analyze.

He said, "What did you think I was going to do?"

The schoolboy's useful, "Uh, nothing, sir," failed me for once. I could not lie to him. I remained silent, partly because the only word I knew for it was too filthy for use outside the barracks.

"I see." He lit another cigarette, and said, "Is it possible that I was preceded by a bad reputation?"

I wanted to laugh. He hadn't a clue to our life. He could have been Jack the Ripper or Alcibiades, as far as his reputation with us was concerned.

He said, "You look amused. Why?"

I told him, beginning to forget again to confine myself to formalities. He took it well enough, but it led him to another question. "Are you so experienced, then, that after one look at me you conclude the worst?"

"No, sir. I'm not experienced at all."

"Who then? Killian?"

I did not want to get Karel into trouble. I said, "It's a camp rule actually. I mean, there isn't much we could do about it anyway, but it all helps."

"You're so elliptical. How does it help?"

I explained it as Karel had explained it to me.

"I see. And who is responsible for this master plan? Killian?"

"I don't know. I didn't come here till two years ago. By then the rules were all established."

"Why is he here? Killian, I mean."

"He published a Communist paper in Prague," I said, this being the most acceptable of Karel's many activities.

"Are you a Communist too, Tyl?"

I said, "Of course," for it had never occurred to me that Karel's friends might hold different politics. Nor, I am certain, had it ever occurred to Karel.

He began to laugh then. "I hope someday you will have the opportunity to tell that to Rittmeister von Pankow."

It was a happy thought. "I hope so too."

He got up and walked to the window, where he stood with his back to the room, looking out over the camp. He said, "Of all the things I hate about my position here, this I hate the most: the unlimited power of being able to say, 'Do this or I will have your head cut off.' "

"Like the Red Queen," I said, remembering a ragged *Alice* with torn pages and *Gabriel von Pankow* written in greasy crayon, each letter a different color, on the flyleaf.

He smiled at that and sat down beside me again. "Tell me, did it never occur to Killian that I would prefer to make my own choice?"

"I suppose he thought you had, when you gave me this job."

"I see. And you? Did you think so too?"

"No. I mean, if you were Gabriel's friend it seems a reasonable thing to do."

"Yes," he agreed and fell silent. That was another danger I began to be aware of, those silences which were not embarrassing but a relaxed, temporary withdrawing from the dialogue to follow some thought of one's own; the kind of silence that covers more than talk can, and which one has no way of countering with a polite formula.

"I don't want it, Tyl."

I shrugged and made a face. It was meant to convey relief within the bounds of politeness, but to be truthful I felt insulted. Probably my face did not turn out as planned, for Svestrom gave me one of those looks I so much disliked; the kind that said I hadn't fooled him. He poured himself another drink and came back to the bed. I knew he was drinking fast to get drunk. He did that often on his bad days.

He said, "Will it get you into trouble with Karel?"

"No. I don't get into trouble with Karel. He's my friend."

"This pandering seems hardly the office of a friend," said Svestrom with distaste.

"I told you. Things are different Inside."

"I do not like your accepting it so matter-of-factly."

"I have to. I am Inside."

"I suppose so. Will everyone in camp be terribly disappointed?"

"Naturally. Everybody prefers a poofed camp commander."

He laughed at that. "Under the circumstances your impudence does you credit, Tyl."

It came to me belatedly that it did not. I couldn't imagine what had made me say such a thing. It was just another example of what Karel called my Prussian stupidity. I said, "I apologize. I forgot the circumstances."

His face, under the scars and the eye patch, was never easy to read. But for some reason my words disarmed its protection; without intending to, I had very much pleased him.

"Dear, dear Tyl. That is the most generous thing anyone has ever said to me. Do you know, sometimes, when you smile, you look very much like Gabriel."

"It's the Pankow face. We all look alike."

"Yes." He was not really listening to me, and though his intimidating pale gaze was on my face, he was not looking at me either. He put out his hand and touched my cheek, a blind man's touch from which I had no impulse to shrink.

He said, "I'll change my mind about this. I do want it."

His touch had been hard and warm and entirely reassuring. His words reminded me of who he was. I said, "You're the camp commander."

It worked. His face went white with anger. He said, "Thank you, Tyl. It wouldn't have done to forget *that*." We were enemies, the only basis on which we might properly communicate.

He said, "Your hands are warm. Aren't you frightened?"

"No." It was the only answer I could make to a taunt. But it was true too. Now that it had come to the point I was only monumentally embarrassed.

"I promise not to hurt you," he said.

"I'm not afraid of you."

"Be still. Close your eyes."

He kept his promise, but it hardly mattered. I had for protection my anger and all my schoolboy nastiness, along with a large amount of schoolboy curiosity. But I quickly found myself bereft of all these weapons by the simple and obvious fact that after all none of this had anything to do with me. There was something of a child dandling a doll, something too of a lover touching the portrait of the person he loves: canvas, not flesh. And as the blind man's touch had not been for me, so neither was any of this.

Afterwards he said, "I wasn't drunk enough," and I found myself wishing I had been able to help him. I wanted to reach out to touch the lank white hair lying tangled on my knee. The intensity of this wish frightened me; I reminded myself again that he was nothing more than the camp commander, nothing less than the enemy.

The unmarked side of his face was turned toward me. I had not realized until that moment, with the ruined part of it out of sight, that he must have been, before the scars, extremely handsome. The fine kestrel profile was marred by the smudges of pain and lack of sleep, the skin lay too tightly on the bones, but it was a face which bore all the markings of strength and beauty. I do not know whether I could have refused anything to the scarred side of his face, but this unconscious perfection stiffened my resolve and kept my hands by my side.

When I left he said, "Don't forget the cigarettes," and at this my anger revived. Had I been braver, I would have thrown them at his face.

I gave the cigarettes to Karel when Jasper came on guard duty. Karel said, "The wages of sin, I presume," which for some reason made me so angry I could not answer.

I turned my back on him, and when in a moment he handed me a lighted cigarette I said, "Fuck off."

He climbed into the bunk beside me and whispered, "Did he hurt you?"

"No."

"It wasn't that bad, was it?"

"Shut up, Karel."

I knew that any of the others, Karel included, in my place would have performed without all this fuss, their feelings uninvolved, treating it as a vaguely unpleasant chore, easier than working in the munitions plant and not nearly as nasty as cleaning latrines. I wanted terribly to be like them, to feel as they did, to be practical and singlehearted.

Karel said, "What's bothering you, Tyl?"

I thought of the nights after the quarry and decided to confide in him. "Karel, what would happen if I got to like him?"

"What, Svestrom?" I could almost see the contemptuous downward turn of his mouth. "Are you screwy? He's the camp commander!"

I turned my face into Karel's shoulder and presently went to sleep. I did not tell him the truth.

Always he said, "Close your eyes," blindly touching my face. I would open them to stare down at the tangle of lank white hair, shuddering at the touch of his mouth on my body. It was not a shudder of revulsion.

"Hold me. Be still. Pretend."

I did as I was told, adding nothing of my own, speaking when spoken to, never touching him unasked, treachery and danger lying on my skin like a tattoo.

God, Karel, you and your technicalities! Why didn't you warn me? Or didn't you know, you so familiar with the body's betrayals; was this one you didn't know about, that Svestrom's whims should so quickly prove to be the precise and specific answer to my needs? I used to wonder about that a lot, those long rainy afternoons I spent silent and hostile in the arms of my enemy.

Svestrom welcomed my silence, I think. It made his own double-dealing easier. For though I did not know it then, he was a double-dealer too. I don't know why one always thinks of the people one deceives as being less complicated. It gives them all the advantage.

But silence and hostility are poor weapons against pain, and he was always in pain. He did not speak of it, but there were mornings when the cigarette ends were high in the ash tray and he had not even made a pretense at going to bed.

He had been unlucky in his doctor. His arm had not healed properly and the bone had set wrong. There is a way of splinting the elbow with steel, an operation my father had been rather famous for. Svestrom's doctor had made no attempt at it. Considering the general clumsiness of his work it was probably just as well.

It was easy to tell the good days from the bad. On his bad days, which grew increasingly more frequent as the filthy weather continued, he wore his arm in a sling and got drunk.

A week of this was enough to exasperate me into breaking my rule of never speaking first. I said, "Isn't there a hospital in Linz?"

He acknowledged my defeat with a smile but was too kind to comment on it. "Surely. Are you feeling ill?"

"Of course not. There are treatments, you know, that would help the pain. Also, it ought to be exercised. Wearing your arm in a sling is about the worst thing you can do for it."

"Heaven forbid. The less I move it the happier it is."

"The less you move it the less you'll be able to move it. You could find a good doctor in Linz."

"I don't want a doctor. Brandy's better."

I poured him a glass. "The doctor that set your arm ought to be court-martialed. He had no business letting you out of the hospital before it was properly healed, for one thing."

"That wasn't his fault. I got bored and left. How do you know so much about these things?"

"I grew up in a doctor's house."

He looked puzzled for a moment. Then he said, "Oh, of course. You mean your father."

"I don't have a father."

He said, quite kindly, "You have a father in Stockholm."

"Screw him."

He put down his brandy and slapped me—with his good hand —hard across the face. I was more startled than angry. Screw you too, I thought, without being able to get up much conviction about it.

"Sorry," he said after a while. "But it is monstrous, you know."

I wondered whether he meant my father's leaving me behind or his slapping me. Either would be acceptable. "What, sir?"

"Your vanity."

"My what?" I was outraged.

"Your vanity, which cannot live with the thought that your family is free while you are a prisoner. It really requires the tribute of all their corpses at Buchenwald, doesn't it? Nothing less will appease it."

"A lot less would have appeased it," I said. "A small effort at the time, for example."

"Perhaps it was made and you don't know about it."

"It wasn't made. I know my family. Effort wasn't their thing."

"Are you sure? It seems impossible that your father didn't even try."

"Oh, he probably went to the consulate in Stockholm, that kind of shit, but he didn't make any efforts that would be a trouble."

"He isn't very much like his brother, then."

"Why?"

"Gabriel was trapped in a burning tank because he tried to get a wounded man out first. He could have jumped clear."

I thought, "I hate you."

"It is the occupational hazard of the tank corps, as drowning is that of the sailor," said Svestrom.

I did not care about the tank corps. Only Gabriel. "Why did you tell me?"

"Because you feel so-o-o sorry for yourself."

I said, "Yes, sir," in my snootiest Rittmeister voice.

"You are angry with me for telling you."

"You're the camp commander. You can say anything you like."

"Yes, it was about time we had that one again. It must be a week since you last mentioned it. Tyl, does it ever occur to you that it's asking a lot of one's parents to expect them to be perfect?"

"I've got out of that habit."

"My father was an opium addict," he said, and added, surprised, "I never meant to tell that to anyone. He was wounded in the last war, and they gave him some at the field hospital. He never got free of it again. It wasn't sordid, you know; he had plenty of money and an understanding doctor. It's only what it does to the personality, a kind of hollowing out; I can't quite explain. The forms stay intact, but there is nothing behind them. We were such an orderly Prussian family, the kind that's such a joke to foreigners and such a comfort to children, with a place for everyone and everyone in his place. Except for the family skeleton walking in the garden and sitting at meals with one. I used to wish he were dead. So you see, I do know how you feel. Believe me, Tyl, as you grow up you stop minding. I did, and you will too. I am sorry I was beastly about Gabriel."

Gabriel and I had come upon a field of poppies once, shimmering in the summer heat. I remembered Gabriel saying, "They make opium from them, you know," and both of us biting into the black seed pods to see what would happen. Nothing had happened. Perhaps they were the wrong kind of poppies.

I told this to Svestrom. He said, "I would never dare to do that. One thing my father did leave me with, a healthy respect for drugs. My doctor gave me a lot of morphine before I left the hospital, but I don't want to use it. It's locked in the bathroom cupboard. I'd love to throw it down the drain, really, but someone in the camp might need it one day. It worries me that there aren't any medical facilities here. What do you do when you get sick?"

"We don't get sick."

"Oh. How do you manage that?"

"This is a labor camp. If you can't work they send you on to places like Buchenwald and Auschwitz, where there are medical facilities."

"I see." He lit a cigarette, handed it to me, lit one for himself, and said, "I will never do that, to anyone here. That's a promise, Tyl. But it worries me, a place like this without any sort of infirmary or anywhere to isolate the sick. I did check into it, in Linz and in Vienna, but they all say they haven't enough medicine for the army, and one can't get building materials. Yet if we empty one of the barracks it crowds the rest so much it's just asking for trouble."

"We've never had anything bad yet." I couldn't see much point in telling him about the man in 4A who had died of peritonitis. It was true enough that bad illnesses were rare with us. I suppose we weren't in good enough shape to be sick. We stayed healthy or we died. "Anyway, you made Four C clean up their mess. That helps."

"That was a favor to me. After all, I lost an eye, not a nose."

Grown careless again, I said, "It's more than Colonel Shit ever did."

"Who?" I knew the moment I said it he couldn't let it pass.

"I'm sorry, I shouldn't have said that. Your predecessor here."

"Why was he called that?"

"Weizeck-*Scheissdreck,* for the rhyme."

"I see. I often wonder about him. What was he like, Tyl?"

I wasn't about to push my chances any further. "All right, I guess."

The slant look, a dubious, "Hm. What happened to him?"

"He committed suicide. He was involved in the July twentieth plot on the Führer."

At this Svestrom said helplessly, "Oh, dear God," and putting his face in his hands laughed until he ran out of breath.

Sleep, my one talent, failed me that night. I could not close my eyes. Behind my lids waited Gabriel, shriveling like carbon paper held to flame. Someone cried out in a nightmare; someone snored. I was used to sleeping in crowds. These things never kept me awake.

Abri said, "What's the matter, Tyl? Can't you sleep?"

"I keep thinking of Gabriel."

"God's messenger, or a friend?"

"My uncle, really. My favorite relation."

"Is he dead?"

"Yes. I knew that. Svestrom told me. He was his battalion commander in Africa. But until today I didn't know how he died."

"How?"

I thought of the flaming synagogue, doors and windows barred. "He was burned alive in his tank." One for the Jews, Abri.

"What was he like, your Gabriel?"

"A daylight person. Joyous. That sounds silly."

Abri lay still, his arms behind his head, his eyes open on the dark, peopled, I was sure, with charred corpses of his own. He said, "I know about daylight people. My father was one. They die young. What would they do with old age?"

"He could have died of a bullet."

"Daylight people belong to the sun. How else should they die but by fire?"

Because it was easier to talk than to be silent, and easier for me to speak of Abri's dead father than of my dead Gabriel, I said, "Abri, why are you—I mean, where were you when the synagogue burned down?"

"At home. I never went to pray. I was already an atheist, you see."

"Didn't your father mind?"

"No, I don't think so. He used to say, 'Every man is both Cain and Abel. That is what the story means.' He believed that everyone's life was a working out of man's relationship to God. How each person worked it out, with prayer, with argument, with negation, or even with madness, that was his own business and to try to interfere was foolishness."

I remembered Sunday morning services in the bright, scrubbed church at home, the Braunsberg schoolmaster both organist and choir—"where'er you walk, cool gales shall fan the glade, trees where you sit shall crowd into a shade"—gillyflowers on the family graves and the pastor for lunch, all of it a pleasant discharging of a weekly duty, no prayer, madness, or indeed God anywhere to be found on the bland Lutheran surface. I remembered too how lightly Abri had turned aside my questions about my becoming a Jew my first winter at the camp. My Jewish Catholic Lutheran mother was no link between us, but the death by fire of a Hasidic scholar in Cracow and a German tank corps captain in Africa had somehow made us brothers.

Abri, the riddle, the one I could never understand. But keep talking, Abri. This is a night I'd as soon talk away. I don't deserve what you're giving me, but I'll take it. I'm not a Jew, Abri. I'm not even a Communist. I'm a Prussian and I take things I don't deserve for the simplest of reasons, because I need them.

Abri continued to talk, but the texture of the night had changed. The noises of the sleepers had grown more insistent, louder, and Abri's voice was low. I could barely hear him.

". . . there was a fire engine in the square. But the SS had their machine guns trained on it. It wouldn't have done any good. They must have drenched the walls with gasoline.

"There wasn't even a cordon to hold people back. The heat did that. It was like a wall. No one could cross it. I know because I tried. It was impossible. But I got close enough to hear the song."

"The song?" I was sure I had not heard him right.

"Yes. They were doing what they had been taught all their lives to do: to sing in the flames until the fire scorched their breath. Now do you understand why I couldn't tell you what a Hasid is, Tyl?"

"I'm sorry I asked you."

"Don't be."

"I don't mean that winter."

"I know what you mean. Don't be sorry. Sometimes it's good to remember. I wish I could remember what the song was. I can't, you know."

"Does it matter? I mean, so long as you know there was a song."

"It should be enough, shouldn't it? Only I keep thinking if I can remember I can stop being afraid."

We are all afraid, of hunger, of cold, of illness, of physical brutality. But I know Abri is not talking about those.

"Afraid of what, Abri?"

Outside a guard walked by, a dog barked. Inside someone snored and coughed, someone else protested against a nightmare. I held my breath and willed the silence to hear Abri's answer. But he only said, "I don't know."

6

On October 14 Fieldmarshal Rommel died, according to the news broadcast, of wounds received earlier in the summer in France, when an American plane had strafed his car. General von Svestrom received this information with a look of icy incredulity. I thought him rather silly. It's true that Rommel was famous for the many hairbreadth escapes that are bound to be the lot of a commander who fights on the front lines and has luck on his side, but though Rommel had been greatly admired, and by some of his officers worshiped, not always this side of idolatry (I am thinking particularly of my uncle Gabriel), surely no one could have supposed him to be immortal.

Svestrom said, "Utter rubbish," and settled down to do some incisive stuff on the telephone which got him through to Herrlingen almost at once, no mean feat the way telephone lines were snarled all over Germany. Of the one-sided conversation I could make little. It consisted mostly of the kind of unfinished sentences people use when they know what they are talking about but don't want anyone else to. Finally he said, "Of course I'm coming to the funeral," and, to some protest at the other end, added, "Well, I prefer being a nettle grasper to being a sitting duck."

When he rang off he became aware of my presence with some annoyance. He said, "I suppose you've been listening."

"Yes, sir. Shall I pack for you?"

"Toothbrush, razor, clean shirt. Just chuck it in the back of the car. I won't be gone long." There was an air about him, a kind of tense cheerfulness.

I put his things in the car and stopped to tell Karel the news of Rommel's death. Predictably, he replied, "That's good."

When I got back to the camp commander's house I saw that he had changed into his best uniform. For the first time he wore all his medals and his seal ring. He said, "All done, Tyl? It took you long enough. Look, I shouldn't be gone more than two or three days, but there's an outside chance I mightn't be back. If so, would you try to send this letter. I know you've got half the guards bribed, and if that doesn't work out, save it till the Russians get here and send it then. It's not urgent." He handed me an envelope. "Good-by, Tyl."

"Good-by, sir."

I watched him as he walked quickly to the car, his leather coat slung over his shoulders. For the first time since the day I had seen him at the edge of the quarry he had again that young man's air about him which had made me mistake his hair for the same tow color as my own. Going to a funeral would hardly give him that look of elation. Danger might, though. What had he meant about not being back?

The Mercedes passed the camp gates. He looked back and gave a brief wave. I went inside the house and looked at the letter in my hand.

> *Frau Baronin von Svestrom*
> *Sandburg*
> *Norden*

So there was one. Well, why on earth not? Lots of people had wives. Why not General von Svestrom?

I wondered what she made of his predilection. Probably she didn't know. He didn't strike me as an indiscreet person. Funny, though.

A *Sandburg* is a sand castle such as children build on the damp edge of the shore, intricate with turrets and casements, to be fetched away by the next tide.

Norden. His home, presumably. A village on the edge of Hanover, across from the Frisian Islands.

Well, no one could have mistaken Svestrom for an adventurer without background. But he had been so completely cut off from this background—by his choice or theirs?—that this sudden acquisition of wife, house, town, and county, the minimums possessed by most people, seemed less a revelation than added mystery. Why was he cut off? Why, before attending Fieldmarshal Rommel's funeral, had he at last written a letter home?

It was one of Karel's theories that where everything is forbidden, everything is allowed. Prisoners therefore were not required to live by ordinary rules.

I took the letter into the kitchen and lit the gas ring under the teakettle. I looked at the address once more, trying to picture the Baronin, and, waiting for the steam, turned the envelope idly in my hand. How easily he had outwitted me. The flap of the envelope was fastened with sealing wax: *A mon seul désir*.

I spent the time General von Svestrom was away lounging on his bed, reading his books, soaking in his bathtub, wasting his coal and hot water with lavishness. I wasn't worried he'd catch me. The muffler on the Mercedes had gotten much worse. It could be heard practically from Linz.

When he had not returned after three days, the luxury of hot baths and illicit BBC broadcasts ceased to comfort me. From Svestrom's desk the sealed letter continued to mock me. Was Svestrom ever coming back?

I told Karel about the existence of the Baronin. He said, "Probably needs an heir," and favored me with a long lecture on the evils of privately owned land and the abuses of a feudal society. It wasn't much help.

"What's the matter, Tyl?"

"Nothing."

"You feeling all right?"

"Sure."

"I miss Svestrom's cigarettes."

"Screw you. I'd rather not have Svestrom's cigarettes and not have Svestrom any day."

"Oh, come on. It's not as bad as all that. Don't tell me you still haven't got used to it."

"Did you, ever?"

"Sure, I told you."

"I meant, did you ever get used to it?"

"There's a lot of worse things, Tyl. I mean, look at it this way, how long does it take? Two minutes and it's done. What's so terrible about it?"

With a physical intuition that was new to me, I guessed that for Karel those two minutes had been the total of his experience. He had never known the leisured, experienced use of another body, never that trap-door drop with not even a noose to hold one up, that racking pleasure which forced me to clench my teeth on my bleeding tongue to keep from crying out.

And lying with my head on Karel's arm, I thought of all the nights he had held me because we were cold or he had the blue devils or I did, and I had never felt more than the warmth and comfort of a friend's body. Unfair, unfair that my enemy had only to put out his hand to turn my bones to water.

I paced the prison rooms of the camp commander's house. At every turn the white rectangle of the envelope mocked my eye.

Was Svestrom never coming back?

He came back after five days and I was glad he did not catch me in the tub or otherwise doing anything illicit, for he was in a flaming rage. I had never seen him so angry before. I couldn't think of anything to say to him. Could I say, "How was the funeral?" as I would say, "How was the play?" Hardly.

I said, "Did you have a bad trip, sir?"

"Oh, hello, Tyl. No, the trip was all right."

"How was the funeral?" Ass!

He looked at me. "Indecent."

I couldn't even think of a stupid comment to make to that. "Shall I get you some dinner, sir?"

"No, thank you, Tyl. One of the Old Faithfuls kindly brought me a fresh supply of brandy from France. I intend to get drunk tonight. Indeed I hope to get blind. If you find me insensible in the morning, please do nothing to revive me. It is the state I hope to achieve."

"All right, sir."

"Why are you smiling?"

He caught me off guard. "I think I am pleased to see you."

"I hope you are properly ashamed of it. Would you like to get drunk with me? It's very good brandy."

"I don't like brandy."

"Barbarian. Run along, then."

"Good night, sir."

"The Führer's wreath," he said, "was so large they had trouble getting it out the door."

I approached his house with caution the next morning. No one wants to disturb a hung-over camp commander. But I did not find him insensible. Indeed, he did not look as if he had slept at all. Unshaven, rumpled, an ash tray overflowing with cigarette ends beside him, he looked as cold sober as the gray October morning. And as cheerful.

"Didn't you make it, sir?"

"The curse of the Svestroms," he said. "A hard head. Well, that's that. The disgraceful end of a great man. How your uncle Gabriel worshiped him. Find me some coffee, Tyl. I'm going to drive into Vienna and requisition blankets for the camp."

I thought they would as soon give him their Aryan hearts' blood, but on second thought I wasn't sure. It would need a brave man to stand up to the look in that pale eye.

After he had gone I noticed that in the wastebasket, torn across and then across again, lay the letter that had mocked me these five days. It was a simple thing to put the four pieces together, and I had no doubt that it implied a gesture of contempt for my nosey-parkering. Had it been important, he would have burned it.

Heiligendorf, October 14.

My dear Karin,

This is the second letter like this I've written to you. If I'm lucky, you'll get this one.

Knowing your fine Spartan attitude of preferring me on my shield rather than with it makes a farewell letter to you delightfully easy to write. I'm off to Rommel's funeral. I would have attended this in any case, out of respect for the best commander I ever served under, but with things as they are, I hope my presence there will force their hand. The situation as it stands now is not tolerable.

I'm sorry you took my not coming home for my convalescent leave (which I didn't take at all) as an insult to you. That was an unlikely sentiment from you, surely. I should have thought the reason would be obvious. I hope the day will never come when the commandant of a concentration camp is welcome at the Sandburg. Though it is my home, this has for the moment to include me.

Perhaps my being at Rommel's funeral will change the status quo into one more satisfactory for both of us. Letters like this, to you, could so easily get to be a bad habit. J.

In the afternoon I took some cigarettes Svestrom had given me and visited Karel's fliers. They had been talking again about escaping, and Karel was worried about them. Four D, where they lived, had been built later than the other barracks and was set back from the camp proper next to a large field full of nettles and dock. The meathooks, which Colonel Shit had moved there, had never been taken down. Nettles and bindweed had almost overgrown them; unless one actually went to the back of 4D they were out of sight of the camp.

I gave John and Peter Svestrom's cigarettes and Karel's message: "Be patient a bit longer."

"Patient up Karel's arse, dear boy," Peter drawled. "It's all we ever are, in full view of those damned meathooks too. Tell Karel that."

I gave them the latest war news hot from the BBC and added

without any particular authority that the war could not last even another half year.

"Who told you, your new pal?"

"You're smoking his cigarettes."

John smiled and said, "The RAF thanks you. Things have eased up for you, haven't they?"

"Yes. About time, too."

Their RAF blues had turned an indefinite color between gray and green. John's were patched, but Peter's hung in rags. He had, however, in spite of his disreputable appearance, been educated at the kind of schools John and Karel were agreed had to be pulled down brick by brick as the first step in the coming revolution—Harrow and Balliol, I think—and he seemed to me the proper person to ask whether he knew a book called *The Portrait of Dorian Gray.*

"*Picture.*"

"No. It's a book."

"I know it's a book, Tyl. It's called *The Picture of Dorian Gray.*"

"Have you read it?"

"Surely. Why?"

"Svestrom has a copy. He reads it all the time. I was just curious about it."

"How very revealing."

"Of what?"

"Well, Dorian Gray is a quite horribly beautiful young man who has his portrait painted by an artist friend. When it is finished he cannot bear the thought that he will grow old and ugly —I must just explain that the author, Oscar Wilde, was a dreadful pansy and liked young men to be very young, very pink, and quite unmarked by intelligence—I've lost track of what I was saying, but in any case Dorian Gray makes the wish that the portrait instead of his own face should show the passage of time. His wish is granted. He never grows old or ugly, and though he leads a dissipated life his face never shows a sign of it. The person in the portrait grows old, evil, and hideous instead.

Remind you of someone who hasn't the benefit of a portrait in his attic?"

"I don't think you're funny," I said, furious.

Peter, his eyes on the gallows, said, "No, I don't think I am."

"They've not been used since he came."

"They can be again, any time."

"No."

"How would you know?"

"I know him, Peter. He would never do anything like that."

"How did he get to be a Nazi general?" John asked.

"John, if I were a bit older, if my father hadn't married a Jew, I'd be in the German army too."

"So?"

"So. Would that make me a monster?"

"Yes."

"I'd still be me."

"To fight for an evil cause is evil."

"Evil is Sunday school rubbish. Nothing is that uncomplicated."

"Not when you need excuses."

"No innocent person was ever hanged because I didn't open my mouth."

The silence that followed this was appalling. I was horrified. I'd never meant to say a thing like that. I hadn't even known that I thought it.

"It will be so nice to get back into polite society," said Peter; "where certain things just aren't said."

"I'm terribly sorry." I really was.

"It's all right," said John. "Do you think it's never on our minds?"

"All the same—"

"Here comes Saint bloody Svestrom."

I turned to watch the Mercedes pull into the camp gates. Svestrom got out, saw me, and began to walk toward us. He returned the two English salutes and said, "Good evening, Tyl."

"Good evening, sir."

"We've got the blankets."

"I'm not surprised."

John and Peter maintained a neutral silence. They were all officers and the forms held. When Svestrom's eye encountered the gallows, I realized that he had probably not been on this side of the barracks before.

He said, "What are those, Tyl?"

"Don't you know, sir?"

He looked surprised at what he no doubt considered an impertinence, though in truth it had been a moment's cowardice, an inability to inflict this on him.

"I asked you a question, Tyl."

"They're butcher's hooks, sir."

"Yes, I can see that. What—"

He'd been about to ask what they were for when it hit him and his mouth closed on the words. John's eyes were on him with pleasure. He said, "They're to hang prisoners from, sir. The prisoners strangle to death very slowly in great pain, and if your tastes lie that way you can watch them. I will say for your predecessor that he didn't go in for that too much; he got his kicks from forcing other people to watch. It was his way of keeping discipline. You can also refuse to let the corpses be cut down. Then the dogs can have their fun. That's kindness to animals. And if things get really boring, you can hang people and cut them down and do it again the next day or the next week. There's a lot you can do, with a little imagination, sir."

Svestrom had listened to this, as if he were under an obligation to hear John out. The scarred, unrevealing side of his face was turned to us. The munitions truck pulled in the gates. Svestrom turned and walked toward it. When he was very tired he dragged his right leg. It was a much older wound than the shattered arm and didn't bother him, as a rule.

I started after him—not knowing what I would do or say when I caught up with him, but feeling I must go—but John caught hold of my wrist and held me back.

"What are you going to do, Tyl, tell him not to worry, he's not to blame for what he inherited from Colonel Shit?"

"Let go, John."

He was a big man. Now he took my other wrist and held them both contemptuously in one hand. He said, "Remember whose side you're on, Tyl."

"Let go!"

"Remember Piers. He was a bit wet, of course, but all the same he was one of us. Remember that we weren't allowed to bury him, and the dogs and the flies."

Svestrom had stopped at the truck. He was counting off the first ten people who got down and giving them instructions. I couldn't hear what he said, but I knew he was ordering the gallows pulled down.

I tried to pull my hands free, but John would not let go. I said, "Of course I remember. I'll probably have nightmares about Piers for the rest of my life. All because he didn't have the guts to survive. And now you remember something, John. I've got a job. I'm out of the quarry and in a job where I can survive. If you want me to lose it, just keep holding on to me."

He dropped my wrists. I had to make an effort not to rub them in front of him. They'd probably be black and blue for weeks. John looked embarrassed, now.

"Sorry, Tyl. I keep losing my temper in this bloody place. I know you're all right. Thanks for the cigarettes."

"You're welcome. Next time you pull this, I'll bite you."

I went back to the camp commander's house. Svestrom was sitting by his desk, his hands before him. He was twisting the seal ring which he was still wearing on his left hand, an empty, absent-minded motion like a prisoner playing with a piece of string. *A mon seul désir.*

He didn't look up when I came in. I didn't know what to do. The scars for once failed to mask his face.

I had never once touched him unasked, and I know I should not have done it then, but despair that is great enough creates its own demands. I put out my hand and touched his. He made no response. Finally he turned his hand, closing his fingers on mine. "Why, Tyl? Why now?"

I betrayed every one of them: the fliers and Piers and the Blitzstein boy and a man called Merz who hadn't enough life left to protest against being hanged from a meathook. I said, "John was wrong. It isn't your fault."

He shook his head. "You're wrong, Tyl."

"They're down now."

"They should never have been up."

It occurred to me that this dialogue would have made more sense if the speakers had been reversed. But I only said, "Could I tell you about the fliers? Maybe you could do something about them."

"Of course. Tell me about the fliers."

"I think they ought to be prisoners of war. Colonel Shit— I'm sorry, Colonel Weizeck—"

"You have my permission to call him anything you please."

"Thanks. Anyway, he got it into his head that they were spies, and I suppose he thought if he got them to confess he'd go to heaven. At first the guards beat them up some and when that didn't do any good—it's my guess they are just shot-down fliers and had nothing to confess; I mean, why should spies be running around in RAF blues, it doesn't make sense—"

"Tyl, is there something that makes it difficult for you to come to the point?"

"Yes."

"The meathooks?"

"Yes."

"Leave it then. Why are two of them left?"

"There were three left, originally. One of them killed himself after a while. I don't know why, exactly. Maybe he couldn't stand the waiting around. Because there was no way of telling with Colonel Shit who would be next, or whether anybody would be. But I don't somehow think it was that, because it happened after Shit had stopped playing games."

"Perhaps he could not bear the guilt of being a survivor."

"I should have thought he'd be grateful."

"Should you? Was it Peter and John who killed Colonel Weizeck?"

"No."

"But somebody did."

"Yes."

"You know who?"

"Yes."

"Would you tell me?"

"No."

"All right. I won't ask you again."

He turned and looked out the window. Rosa was hunting, lean and red, in the draggled grass. She startled a lark. It flew straight up and presently forgot the danger and began to sing.

"Those larks," said Svestrom, "are a great compensation for insomnia. I always watch them at dawn."

I too had watched the larks many mornings, soaring past the barbed wire, trailing their song above the camp. I said, "I hate the bloody bastards."

He did not turn from the window. Rosa was teasing a field mouse. Svestrom said, "If that is not monstrous vanity. Even the larks must be grounded because Tyl Pankow is not free."

I had seen this in him before, this capacity for extremes. "Gallows and larks," I said. "I can't do those sudden jumps."

"I know. I seem to have a talent for the trivial. Had I been Faust—Goethe's Faust, I mean—I would have lost my soul the first day."

"Why?"

"Goethe's Faust doesn't just sign his soul away at the end of twenty-five years, the way Dr. Faustus in the legend does. He hedges his bargain. He says if the devil can provide him with an experience which will make him say to a single moment: 'Stay, you are so beautiful,' the devil can have his soul from that moment. Of course he never does, and Faust keeps his soul. I must admit that there haven't been many days in my life that the devil didn't provide me with at least one moment I could say that to."

I said, "It's easier the other way."

"All larks or all prison? I imagine so."

My hand was still in his, scarred from the quarry, grubby, the nails bitten raw. He opened his fingers and laid it against his face. He said, "Stay here with me tonight, Tyl."

I wanted to say yes so much the sheer magnitude of the wish was a betrayal.

He said, "I need company. I can get through the days, but I can't take the nights any longer. I drink and drink and it doesn't do any good. I'm sick to death of it."

I know, I told him silently. I lie in my bunk, smoking your cigarettes, listening to Karel's stories, and I'm here every night. It's you I see, crippled and drunk and exhausted. I know how you spend your nights, waiting, waiting for the time to pass, waiting for the Russians to get here so you'll be free to reach for your gun and pull the trigger. Oh, yes, I know. I think I knew it even before I'd read your letter. I don't know anything else about you, not why you're here or why you've chosen to stay, but I do know this: you're the most desperate prisoner in this camp.

I said nothing.

He said, "If you're worried about your reputation I'll be glad to make it an order."

I said the first thing that came into my head. "Prisoners don't have a reputation. I was thinking of yours."

"Mine? My reputation?" He began to laugh. "The commandant of a concentration camp! Dear God, Tyl, what kind of reputation do you think I have left?"

John and Peter were transferred to a POW camp a week later. They stopped at 4A to say good-by.

"I take it we owe this to your good offices," said Peter to me. "The RAF thanks you."

"We'll see to it you get the DFC," said John.

Like a fool I asked, "What's a DFC?"

"Distinguished fucking cross," said Karel. He was angry with me. "Good-by, John, Peter. I wish there were eight of you leaving." He saluted them with his closed fist.

We watched them out of the camp gates in silence. I was damned if I spoke first.

Karel touched my shoulder. "I'm sorry, Tyl."

"What the hell do you want me to do, say no thanks to the camp commander?"

His arm tightened on my shoulder. I put my face against his sleeve to hide my lying eyes. I thought, You wanted me to be a whore. I'm nothing you didn't want for me—and knew it to be a lie. Whores fake passion. I faked indifference, growing less expert with practice, not more. It hardly seemed to matter now, compared to the other betrayal. A burglar putting a coin in the poor box, that was what all the fuss about sex amounted to.

I loved Johannes von Svestrom, the camp commander, Colonel Shit's successor. I shared his nights, his bed, his cigarettes, his blind, impatient panic for morning; I accepted like water in the desert his tenderness, his mockery, his expert, untender passion. My silence had maneuvered him into giving me the order to stay with him, but I knew that had I said, then or at any time, "Let me go. Send me back to my side. You can find someone else. The camp's full of people who'd do it gladly for a piece of bread or a pair of shoes. They're safe. They're in no danger. I am. I do it for nothing," he would have sent me away.

My traitor's eyes hidden against the rough denim of Karel's sleeve, I knew that I no longer had any right to his friendship and protection, and knew that I could not do without them and would cheat and lie to have them as I cheated and lied to have Svestrom.

I had taken possession of the one place which no one may claim in time of war: the middle ground between opposing camps.

7

Winter always came too early at Heiligendorf. Of my three winters there the last one was the most tolerable, not only for me but for everyone in the camp. Svestrom had managed to get extra blankets and there was more food. He also allowed us out into the woods surrounding the camp to gather pine cones and fallen tree branches, which we could burn in old petrol tins with holes punched in their sides. The guards were annoyed about this; they said it was hard to keep an eye on us in the woods and we would escape. Svestrom said, "Where would they escape to, with not even an overcoat to their names?" Some of the stupidest prisoners did in fact escape. They were promptly brought back by the local farmers. There used to be a reward for escaped inmates in Colonel Shit's day. All the farmers got from Svestrom was a nasty look.

In the barracks we piled our blankets together and slept again three and four to a bunk for warmth. But I should not say "we." Most nights I slept in a bed with a proper mattress and clean sheets, warm in the arms of my enemy.

There was of course no Christmas in the camp. Many of the inmates were Jews, and the ones who weren't held that it was the opium of the people. At home we had always had a bang-up Christmas with too many presents and too many sweets. I preferred it the way it was done at the camp. But for some reason I wanted terribly to give Svestrom a present.

The camp kept its own anniversaries and kept them in silence.

December 23 was the day a man had been shot for snatching a piece of bread from Colonel Shit's hand.

I went into the garden to the corner where the clumps of hellebores grew under the snow. I brushed the snow away and they were there: a wintertime miracle year after year. I broke them off and put them in water in the camp commander's living room.

Svestrom noticed them the moment he came in. "Christmas roses. Where did you find them, Tyl?"

"They're from the garden. Colonel Shit grew them."

He touched the cold, white petals. "They are beautiful, nevertheless. I love all the flowers that grow at the wrong time of the year: cyclamen and winter aconite and yellow jasmine. And flowers that grow in the desert. In the spring you cannot see the sand for the flowers in North Africa."

The day before Christmas, Svestrom's Mercedes pulled into the camp gates with a passenger in the back seat: a trussed and very irate pig. The guard at the gate was so startled he forgot to salute. In a moment there was such a crowd around the car I couldn't see what was happening. Presumably the pig was unloaded with difficulty. When Svestrom at last walked into the house he went first to wash. "A smelly creature," he said. "Didn't he look exactly like Goering in the back seat of the car?"

"How on earth did you get him?" I knew the farmers had for months absolutely refused to accept money for meat. They could do so much better on the black market.

"I promised they could have the Mercedes the day the war ends," Svestrom said. "It belongs to the army, not to me, but that will be irrelevant by then. It needs a new muffler and they have to paint over the swastika on the door, but apart from that it's a damned good car and well worth a pig. And we will not eat mouse sausage for Christmas dinner."

"I used to be very fond of pork chops," I said.

Within half an hour Svestrom's Christmas gift had split the camp in a quarrel more fierce than any we had ever had. Little

Rosenblum, the butcher (he was four foot eight, as compared to big Rosenblum, the barber, who was five foot two), refused absolutely to touch the pig. Though threatened by a group of Communists and quite a few Jews, and supported only by a much smaller group, he was standing his ground with a courage worthy of a better cause. Karel was threatening exotic tortures, but Rosenblum was unmoved. "You want it dead," he said, "you kill it."

The pig looked at Karel. Karel backed.

"Tyl!"

"Tyl, this fucking bastard won't kill the pig. He says it's not kosher, of all the fucking stupid remarks—"

"Tyl, at least half of us couldn't eat if we have pork."

"Good. More for us."

"Tyl, you've got to tell the general. It's not fair."

"Come and tell him yourself."

"No, thanks, not me."

"If you're not afraid of Karel, and you're not afraid of that pig, you shouldn't be afraid of General von Svestrom. He's much less dangerous."

One of Rosenblum's supporters informed Karel that swine did not chew the cud. Karel said he didn't care.

"Oh, come on," I said. "You can tell him, Rosenblum." It was mean of me, for I knew Rosenblum was frightened, but I had been looking forward to those pork chops. "Come on."

Shaky, but with a martyr's determination, little Rosenblum separated himself from his supporters and came with me. Out of the corner of my eye I caught Karel's grin and his up-yours gesture.

Svestrom, who had apparently heard the commotion, met us outside his house. "What is going on, Tyl?"

Because I could not forgive the loss of pork chops, I refused to speak for the others. "Rosenblum has a problem, sir."

"Well, Rosenblum?"

"Sir, General Camp Commander, sir—" Rosenblum involved himself in a web of titles. The slightest upslant of brow and mouth betrayed Svestrom's effort not to smile. I tried to see him as the others did; the severe officer in his Nazi uniform, formidably, hatefully Prussian, the man who held the power of life and death. They all knew by now that he would not use it, but they continued to be afraid of him; even the guards, even Karel. I remembered the taste of his kiss and his scarred body at the mercy of mine.

"I am sorry, Rosenblum, that was silly of me. I should have remembered. What can you eat?"

"Beef, veal—just not pork, General Camp Commander, sir."

"Very well, let's see what we can do."

They went together to inspect the pig. I went inside the house. Svestrom came in an hour or so later. When he had shut the door he at last gave way to mirth.

"We now own an elderly steer," he said. "It seems to be satisfactory to everyone, and I must say he had a much nicer disposition than the pig. Silly of me, I should have remembered."

I said, "Don't look at me. The Elies were Catholics, you know, and I never even met a Jew till I came to Heiligendorf. Pork chops are my favorite food."

He said, "I know everyone is a Jew or a Communist or both, but it is Christmas Eve. Wouldn't you like to spend it with your friends, Tyl?"

I wouldn't. I would one thousand times rather have spent it with the camp commander. The realization was so sudden that I had no time to protect myself from it. I could only cheat.

"Thank you, sir. I'd love it."

"Run along, then."

"Good night, sir."

"Oh, Tyl—"

I let go of the doorknob. Had he changed his mind?

"Here, catch."

He threw me a pack of cigarettes. Full, unopened. They had become an exceedingly rare luxury; I hadn't seen any in weeks. Svestrom rolled his own, with loose tobacco that smelled like damp hay.

"Have a nice evening."

"Thank you, sir."

I walked across the icy camp yard and opened the door to 4A. It was dark in the barracks. Karel and the Reds were hunched over a pine-cone fire in a petrol tin, doing what savages have always done during long winter nights: telling stories.

Karel looked up, annoyed at the draught of cold air. "What the fucking hell—Tyl! You've got the night off." His bear hug nearly cracked my ribs.

I gave him the cigarettes. "Merry Christmas from General von Svestrom, Karel."

"Christmas," said Abri, "is the nicotine of the people."

Karel, who hated puns, aimed an absent-minded kick at Abri. They shifted, opening their circle to make room for me. Under the blankets, with Rosa and her latest offspring, Marx, to warm our feet, we lit cigarettes, and Abri resumed his story.

"It was already eleven o'clock, and the Italian still had not arrived. There was an old woman, praying, and the limping verger, and at a small side altar a priest who seemed to be about to preach a sermon in the dark, empty cathedral. But when he began to speak he did not address a nonexistent congregation. He was calling, loudly and unmistakably: 'Joseph K.!'"

I felt as if I had never been away. I was not a visitor but the link of a chain. Karel was on my right, his arm thrown across my shoulder. Dieter, vague and amiable, smiled across the pine-cone flame, and Abri, his beautiful face bent down to light a cigarette, suddenly smiled too. I would not, I told myself, choose to be anywhere else. Not in the circle of another arm, lame and brittle-boned, without weight on my shoulder. Not across from a scarred face smiling suddenly from the shadow of a lit match. Not listening to another tale ("Then Marcel, in a great rage, stamped the Baron's top hat quite flat—"). Oh, poor darling Tyl, who can't have his cake and eat it.

" 'You are an accused man,' said the priest.

" 'Yes,' said K. 'So I've been informed.' "

" 'Then,' said the priest, 'I've been looking for you. I am the prison chaplain.' "

"Pull your claws in, you bastard," said Karel, and removed Marx, who had been climbing up the inside of his trouser leg. We loved Rosa because she was scruffy, ugly, and ours. Marx was something else again. Marx was special. During Rosa's last absence (she often disappeared for weeks at a time, causing Karel to observe that Heiligendorf was too fucked up even for alley cats) Rosa had evidently encountered a tomcat of breeding, for she had borne a single kitten who combined, with Rosa's marmalade coat, the dark mask and paw shadings, and the amethyst eyes, of a Siamese. He was an exceedingly odd-looking cat, and much the handsomest we had ever seen.

There was no question of eating him. The rabbi issued a formal complaint that (a) the barracks smelled like a zoo—true, but entirely due to the presence of sheenies, according to Karel, (b) the cats were eating food that should rightly have gone to humans—true, (c) the cats were unsanitary—false. Karel received all complaints pleasantly, pointing out merely that he ran 4A and that anyone who cared to challenge his position had only to try.

Thinking it would please him I suggested we call the kitten Trotsky, but all I got for my pains was the remark that my political orientation was totally fucked up, and a long lecture. In the end the kitten was named Marx.

I had an idea. I said, "Karel, Svestrom's house has mice. Why don't we give him Marx? He could get fattened up a little."

Karel ran a finger down the skinny ribs, starting up a rumbling purr. "I guess he could do with a mouse. If you want to give a cat called Marx to a Nazi general, go ahead."

I took Marx to the camp commander's house the next morning. Svestrom was out. Marx stuck close to my heels for half an hour or so, then began to explore, and had soon located his first mousehole. By noon he had fought with and left in shreds a curtain, two shoelaces, and a requisition form from the munitions factory, and I was beginning to have doubts about the suitability of my gift. By the time Svestrom came in, Marx had caught, teased and killed his first mouse. He laid the mangled body at Svestrom's feet by way of introduction.

"Good heavens, Tyl."

"It's a cat, sir."

"Yes, I can see it's a cat."

"And a dead mouse."

"I can see that too." He bent down and rubbed Marx between the ears. Marx responded with a blue-eyed squint.

"What an odd-looking cat. Would she be part Siamese?"

"It's a he. We don't know who the father is. We thought if you'd like him we would like you to have him."

"We?"

"Me. And Karel and the others."

Marx walked up the black uniform sleeve, wrapped himself into a ball, and went to sleep.

"He is certainly a very confiding cat."

He was a confiding cat. He would do for me what I was not allowed to do. Though I doubted that Svestrom would recognize in a kitten called Marx a cipher for my affection.

"I hope you like cats," I said belatedly.

"Yes. In Africa we had a tiger cub."

"Did you? What happened to it?"

"I couldn't housebreak it and it got too big to spank."

"This tiger's housebroken. Rosa trained him."

"Good. Has he a name?"

"Don't you want to name him yourself?"

"Not if he already has a name."

"It's Marx."

"Good heavens. Why?"

"Well, Rosa used to be called Lenin until she got pregnant, so then we called her after Rosa Luxemburg."

"At least you didn't call her Krupskaya."

"What's that?"

"Frau Lenin. A good Communist like you should really know that."

"Yes, sir."

"And Tyl—"

"Yes?"

"Do you think that when we are alone you could stop calling me sir? After all, I do, like the cat, have a name."

"I know. Johannes."

"I've always been called that. Not Hans or Hannes or anything."

I knew I would never call him Johannes. I had lost so much ground already, I could not afford to surrender even one more of my defenses.

Christmas was one of our good days. There were others. For we were never alone. There was always a third between us: the radio. And that winter the wraps came off the camps in the east, the real ones, whose business was the manufacture of death. Belsen, Treblinka, Auschwitz: at Heiligendorf names to threaten the disobedient and careless, vague places of terror, hell for sinners. Like hell they had no reality that could be grasped.

The Russians changed that. They did not deal in allegory. They unlocked a charnel house and described what they saw.

Svestrom and I listened, the radio between us on the table. I had no wish to hear it, but he did not put out his hand to turn the dial and I could not do it for him. For once he failed to use even the defense so habitual to him, the scar-marked side of his face turned to anyone watching him. He listened, open to any attack, anything I might say to him to flay the skin from his nerves. But there was nothing I wanted to say. I was as far removed from it as he was. One could only be part of it or an outsider. Heiligendorf was as far outside as the German army.

There is so much more now than in that first, crude, shocked newscast. There are films and photographs and trial testimonies and statistics. There is in fact, as there already was that primitive first time, too much. It is too large and affords no handhold. Auschwitz is an abstraction. It has come to be a cipher for all the others. Auschwitz means Belsen and Treblinka, Buchenwald and Dachau, means all of them and none. Its reality exists as a symbol only, an insurmountable road block lying across civilization.

8

On the north side of the camp commander's house an icicle hung from the gutter. It was as long as and considerably fatter than my arm, and served as my weather indicator. Days when it dripped were tolerable. The others were not.

Late in March the icicle began to shrink. The wind was tangibly warmer, blowing across the mountains from the south. The icicle, though on the shady side of the house, continued to drip, the snow grew soft, and water began to seep into the barracks.

There would be frosts still and icy nights, but we were past the worst and had survived another winter.

This was never a time for rejoicing and gratitude. It was a time for *cafard,* headache, itching chilblains, snapped tempers, and violent quarrels. It was also the most dangerous time for typhus, when sanitary arrangements, treated with negligence through the months of hard frost, made themselves unmistakably plain.

On a day in late March, a day of brilliant sun, mud to the knees, and intolerable chilblains, Svestrom came in from his inspection of the camp. All the barracks were flooded. Svestrom was wet and muddy and sufficiently annoyed to say that if typhus were not a contagious disease he wished the Menshevik in 4C would get it.

"I've got Killian standing over him while he cleans up the mess," he said. "It seems to be the only way. I think it's going to turn colder again. A frost for a night or two would be a help. Damn it, Tyl, stop scratching your fingers. They're a bloody enough mess now."

"They itch." I was glad he had given Karel a job. Karel had been headachy, remote, and unapproachable the last week. I blamed it on the south wind and hoped that being in charge while the Menshevik shoveled shit would cheer him up.

"I've got the water hot if you want a bath, sir."

"I thought I told you not to waste coal, Tyl. If I had any strength of character I'd punish you."

He took off his leather coat and began to unbutton his tunic. He managed everything well enough with one hand, but the small hooks at the collar gave him trouble. I reached up to help him.

He said, "You spoil me, Tyl. How will I ever manage without you?"

I said nothing. I hated that kind of conversation. He handed me the coat. "See if you can get some of the mud off this." He went into the bathroom. I emptied his pockets: loose change, tobacco and cigarette papers, matches, a single leather glove. (*'Il m'en restait un seul. Je l'ai laissé dans la figure de quelqu'un.'* Monsignor Hesbach had taken me to see *Cyrano* once. I'd loved it.) I knew the contents of Svestrom's wallet, of course. I'd been through it. Identity card (Major General Johannes Quentin von Svestrom, born July 28, 1911, Norden, Hanover), driver's license, some money. No photographs, no letters. I'd been through everything.

No, not quite everything. The Afrika Korps jacket had hung undisturbed at the back of the closet since Svestrom had put it there.

One hell of a spy I'd make.

I pushed the other uniforms aside and took out the brown tunic with the captain's badges. The pockets were empty except for a thin book. It was in English and had the unsatisfactory name: *Last Poems*. I turned the pages. A line here and there made sense. Some of the poems were so simple even my English was sufficient.

"To think that two and two are four, and neither five nor three, the heart of man has long been sore and long is like to be." I could understand that one.

I turned to the title page and my own name leaped out at me before I found the author's. G. v. Pankow. The book was Gabriel's.

People borrow books, of course. And if the owner is burned to death in his tank in the meantime it is difficult to give them back. People even steal books. Gabriel always did. From ships' libraries and rented summer cottages and doctors' waiting rooms. "I can't bear to think of them so neglected," he used to say by way of excuse.

There was a letter in *Last Poems* too. A letter and a photograph. The photograph was at a guess three years old, which took us back into the distant past when Germany was winning the war, Tyl Pankow was still at St. Pölten, and the Afrika Korps was doing fine in the desert.

Two of its officers had had their picture taken, one leaning from the turret of his tank, dust goggles pushed above the brim of his cap, field glasses slung around his neck: Gabriel, laughing and happy. The other, standing on the desert sand, looking not much older, though he wore the rank badges of a colonel, smiling, squinting a little against the sun with two good eyes: Johannes von Svestrom.

It was not a specially good picture. The sun was too bright and the two had not bothered to look toward the photographer, had probably been scarcely aware that the picture was being taken, having other things to laugh about. Their pleasure in each other's company was the most tangible thing in the photograph.

I turned it in my hand. There was a date written on the back: 15 June 1942. One week before Gabriel's death, a month before my arrest.

I had spent June of '42 with Monsignor Hesbach, sailing on the Wörthersee. Gabriel had blown in for an afternoon's visit, looking to my dazzled eyes devastatingly handsome in his Afrika

Korps uniform, talking a blue streak, sailing our boat with a competence that took my breath away, laughing and joyous, on the verge of an explosion into ecstasy.

Monsignor Hesbach left us alone on a hill above the lake in the afternoon, saying he had letters to write.

"What a good sort," said Gabriel. "I didn't know people still said they had letters to write when they're being tactful."

"He also says he has to wash his hands when he really has to pee, but he is a good sort."

The grass was so high on the hillside that when I lay back it closed above me and I saw the blue sky through a tracery of slender seed pods and dark green fronds.

"Are you on leave, Gabriel?"

"Till tonight. I can't wait to get back, to tell you the truth. But I did just want to see you were looked after all right."

"Yes, fine, thanks. Is it so much fun, the tank corps?"

For one moment he had looked as if he did not know what I was talking about. Then he said, "Oh, yes, the tank corps. Yes, it's lots of fun."

"Did you go to Pankow for your leave?"

"Yes." He pulled his face into a Rittmeister grimace and added, "I left Under A Cloud." He turned in the tall grass, laughing down at me, his eyes as blue as the mountain sky. "Father had a wife picked out for me."

"Was she ugly?"

"No. Quite pretty, in fact, and very rich."

"Why did you refuse her?"

"I had to. You see, I'm in love with someone else."

"Oh, Gabriel." I thought it terribly romantic and very proper for him. "Will you marry the other one, the one you're in love with?"

He smiled and shook his head. "No, Tyl. Too many complications."

These complications did not weigh on him, however. He jumped up, pulled me to my feet, swung me in the air, hugged me till my ribs cracked. "Crazy! Be pleased for me, Tyl."

I had said, "I am," which was true.

I unfolded the letter. It was only a last page, in Gabriel's writing. But I knew to whom it was addressed.

. . . mine. A lack, not a virtue. Indifference rather than generosity. (At my confirmation my parents gave me a watch that was an instrument panel of things, any boy's delight. When it in turn began to delight my nephew, it seemed the obvious thing to give it to him. Both my parents, to my bewilderment, were extremely hurt by this. Do you understand?)

I was the nephew. I had cherished the watch until Mauthausen, where it had in turn become the delight of one of the guards.

All this has now changed, and I want to say "mine" about the one thing no one can own: another person, you. If I were not so happy I would be terrified.

In exchange I can only give you another word that has had no meaning until now, though I always obediently signed it to my letters.

Yours, Gabriel.

"—because you are your Uncle Gabriel's nephew, as a flagrant case of nepotism—"

"Close your eyes. Pretend." Of course.

Gabriel, the one Pankow I would have sworn would never hurt me.

Gabriel, who had given me Svestrom.

I had always thought of it like that, the act of kindness past death. Now he had reclaimed him. No, that was vanity again. There was nothing to reclaim. I had never owned a thought or breath of him, only a Pankow face, a Pankow voice, Pankow tricks of speech. There was no Tyl, not even Tyl the prisoner, only a body that could be made to serve for another. The rest existed in my imagination alone. The things which had assumed such necessity in my life that to have them I daily betrayed my friends, my side and its dead, were creatures of my vanity: the possession of a dead man.

I looked down at the photograph. But Gabriel had no answer for me. Standing in the turret of the tank which was so soon to become his flaming stake and scaffold, his laughter and glance were for the man who now stood looking down at me. How long, I wondered. I had not heard the water stop running.

He held out his hand for the book. He did not look angry, only very tired.

"You and Gabriel—"

He smiled. "This is late in the day. You're not a very efficient snoop, are you?"

"No, sir."

"Why do you look like that? Does it seem so surprising?"

"No." And why the hell should I be surprised? I didn't mean enough to my own father for him to care whether I lived or died, why should I expect to be anything more than a stand-in for Gabriel to you? "I knew in a sort of way. Gabriel visited me that June. I mean, I knew he was in love. It didn't occur to me at that time that he was a—" I could not say it. I could use the word of Svestrom and myself, but not of Gabriel.

It was understandable that Svestrom should misinterpret my misery, but intolerable that he should be kind.

"Don't mind so much about Gabriel, Tyl. It wasn't what you are thinking. We loved each other. We were very happy, both of us."

God, don't you think I know? That's what I can't stand. Do you think I give a damn about whatever back-alley screwing you've done? I loved Gabriel. I loved him so much that day. He didn't even know I was alive. All he could think of was getting back to you.

Svestrom said, "Two years. Does it seem a long time to you?"

"Depends on what you're doing." I had been at Heiligendorf almost three. "It's not so bad, two years of being first in somebody's life."

He sat down at the edge of the window sill and took the photograph from my fingers. "That's true."

Words are the only weapon a prisoner has. I said. "After Gabriel, how can you be satisfied with this?"

"This?"

"Me. Like sleeping with whores and pretending in the dark they're someone else."

He did not bother to deny my status. He said, "I don't think I've ever said that I found it particularly satisfactory, though not precisely for that reason. Anyway, I might as well get used to it, unless I expect to lead a celibate life. Look at me, Tyl. Who do you think would have me for love now?"

Because he had never seemed ugly to me it had not occurred to me that he thought so of himself. It took an act of imagination of which I was not capable to step into his skin, to see, as he saw every day, a crippled body and ruined face.

I don't know—how can I know?—what I would have felt for the handsome young colonel in the photograph. Nothing special, I suspect. It was the Dorian Gray face, half demon, half god, the white hair that should have been tow, the botched surgeon's work on the fine bone and good skin, the ruined angel look that I had loved from the first.

I said nothing. If he thought himself a monster it was a fair punishment for having loved Gabriel instead of me.

Darkness had come into the room while we talked. I heard the van down by the gates and moved to leave. I wanted to run to Karel, the person for whom *I* came first. I wanted to hear his stories about the Menshevik shit, his awful, dull lectures about the differences between Trotsky and Stalin. I said, "Please, sir, can I go now?"

The camp commander could have ordered me to stay. But we were long past that. He looked up, thoughtful and a little puzzled, and said, "Yes, of course, if you want to, Tyl."

The temperature had dropped outside. My feet crunched on newly frozen ice and my breath stood white in front of my face. I ran because I was cold and in a hurry to get to Karel, for whom I was Tyl, not a stand-in for Gabriel, not Gabriel, not Gabriel, not Gabriel.

I forced myself to stop running. I said out loud, "I am Tyl." Nothing is more easily lost to the prisoner than his identity, and there is no easier way of losing it than by identifying himself in terms of who he is not.

9

I pulled open the barracks door.

That fear has a recognizable smell, animals and people in constant danger know. With a prolonged education it becomes possible to sniff out different kinds of fear: the blood stench which panics animals in the slaughterhouse, the stone-dust smell of madness, the mildew stink of death from starvation. These I knew. This I did not.

The rabbi and his group against the farthest wall, four Reds across the room, the fifth in his bunk, the blanket kicked off, warm with fever and vague with headache.

I ran to him, snatching a candle from someone's hand. His skin was stained with the mulberry-colored bruises that left no doubt.

"Karel, oh damn you!"

He turned his head, squinting painfully into the candle. I moved it out of his sight.

"Fuck off, Tyl."

His tongue was dry and crusted. He could barely speak. I got our tin cup and filled it with water. I couldn't remember whether water was bad for typhus or not, but I knew that if it killed him I would not have had the courage to refuse it to him.

"Fuck off," Karel growled again. "You know this is catching."

He needed an ice bag. Even a cloth filled with snow would do. But there was no cloth, not even a rag. I looked up and at last recognized the smell in the room: disaster and unrelenting hostility.

In a prison camp, anywhere where there is no possibility of isolating the sick, there is only one way to deal with typhus. It is inhuman, but the survival of the rest of the people in the camp depends on it. It was always done like this. I knew it from Karel. You drew straws, and the two people who lost took the sick man and carried him to the farthest end of the camp, as far from the barracks as possible, and left him there to die. It was the only thing to do, and Karel's brother, Karel's friends, had not allowed it.

The rabbi took a step forward and said, "I'll help you carry him, Tyl." It was brave of him, braver than he knew. If I had had any kind of weapon, I would have killed him.

I said, "Fuck off, rabbi."

He took another step toward me.

I said, "Touch Karel, and I'll make you wish you were dying of typhus instead of what I'm going to do to you. And that goes for all you sheenies. You don't like the air in here, sleep outside."

It was the idlest of threats. There wasn't a thing I could do to him, and there were thirty of them against the five of us. But he stepped back. His look of hatred said everything he did not have the nerve to say: that I was the camp commander's whore, and for this and my whim death would threaten everyone in 4A and the camp.

I said, "Give me your shirt."

He took it off and handed it to me without a word. I tore out a sleeve and threw it back to him. "Thank you."

He didn't have enough fight left in him not to say, "You're welcome."

I said, "Watch him, Paul," and went outside to fill the sleeve with snow. With the ends tucked under it made an acceptable ice bag.

Franticek came outside and squatted down beside me. He said, "Tyl, please let me help you."

"There's no point to that."

"He's my brother. Tyl, I don't want to keep away. It was only that first moment. I panicked for a minute."

I knew what he meant. I was beginning to feel it myself. Typhus. The worst that could happen in camp. The only comparison I can think of for Outside would be cancer, if that were a contagious disease.

Franticek had had his moment of fright and had reconsidered. I had not considered at all and had mine now. He was braver than I. But it was done and could not be reversed.

"Franticek, you've been around the camps. Do you know anything about typhus? Is water all right?"

"You're the doctor's son."

"Hell, he had a society practice. People like that don't get typhus."

"Nussbaum in Four C used to be a doctor."

"He wouldn't come. Anyway, I don't want it to get out about Karel. They'd make us put him outside. I can't terrorize the whole camp."

"You're doing all right. Must be your *Junker* blood."

"What about soup? The kitchen smelled like the place where the old horse died, earlier this afternoon. Rosenblum must be making horse-meat soup."

"I'll get you some. It should be all right. Our mother always made chicken soup when we were sick."

Karel was delirious through the night. He asked for water but could not keep the soup down. I knew the drinking water ought to be boiled, but there wasn't anything I could do about it. I sat beside Karel's bunk through the night, wrapped in my blanket, falling asleep occasionally, my head against a wooden slat. Karel recognized me sometimes, then he swore and told me to go away, but most of the time he accepted the water in a feverish stupor. I hoped he felt as vague as he looked.

I had threatened Martin Lenz with every imaginable torture if he told Jasper about Karel. He said, "I wouldn't have anyway," and apparently he kept his word, for no one came to bother us.

In the morning Karel's fever did not go down. Paul brought me a cup of acorn coffee and two slices of bread which I could not swallow. Apparently our threats still held good, for everyone went off in the van except the people who had jobs in the camp.

My own comings and goings were never much remarked upon; everyone knew my hours were peculiar, and I was not missed at breakfast. Paul said they'd managed to cover up for Karel at the morning *Appell*.

In the distant pre-camp past, when such things had existed, I had seen a Garbo film (she was the first great passion of my life) in which she had run away from her husband with a maharajah or something but had returned to the husband when he was fighting a typhus epidemic and caught it himself. I was trying to remember what she had done, medically speaking, but could only recall that she had looked smashing with her hair done up in a coif. I wasn't even sure it was typhus. It might have been cholera.

I could not see ahead. How long could such a thing be kept secret? How long before someone else got it?

I was tired and frightened and thinking in circles, getting no answers, only more questions.

"Tyl?"

The black uniform outlined against the light in the doorway, the eye patch and white hair: my well in the desert.

"Please, don't come in here, sir."

I saw him move. Take a step forward.

"No, please. Karel's ill."

He walked forward and stood beside the bunk, looking down. "Is it typhus?"

"Yes."

Karel stirred and opened his eyes. "Fuck off."

I said, "He's delirious, sir."

With the worried frown still between his eyes, Svestrom smiled. "So I imagined. We can't leave him here, Tyl. It isn't fair to the others. We'll take him to my house."

"But, sir—"

"What were you planning to do with him? Leave him in a barracks with forty other people? Come, we can carry him in the blanket. That way I can manage with one hand." He looked around, thinking of what he must do. Then he kicked the water bucket over, making sure all the water ran out. He went to the doorway, called the guards and told them we had typhus in the camp, but gave them no time to panic. He assigned one guard to empty all the water buckets, another to go to the kitchen and make sure the drinking water was boiled, assigned some workers to get the coal from his cellar to use in the large boiler, and set the others to work with kettles and carbolic. Of this we had a large supply, fortunately.

It was the first time I had ever seen Svestrom cope with an emergency. He was marvelous.

We carried Karel to the camp commander's house. He resented this strongly and cursed loudly. Svestrom said, "He almost sounds as if he were feeling better. You'd better strip his bunk, Tyl, and get everything boiled in carbolic. Take this blanket, too. He can have mine in the meantime. I'll be over to give you a hand in a moment."

I wasn't crazy about him handling Karel's things, though it probably wasn't any worse than having a typhus patient in the house.

"I can manage, sir."

"All right. Get going."

Whether it was the proper bed or merely part of the illness, Karel seemed better after he was moved. He managed to keep down some soup and was fairly clear in his head. When I told him where he was I thought for one moment he'd get up and walk out.

In the evening the munitions workers returned to a camp reeking of carbolic (who would ever have thought of it as a comforting smell?) and to an incisive camp commander who herded everyone into the heated dining hall, had every shred of clothing boiled in a cauldron which, judging by the smell, was filled to the brim with straight carbolic, had the camp barber set to work on Menshevik hair and orthodox beards, and had everyone clean, unlousy (hopefully), and fed by ten o'clock. He had taken my own uniform earlier in the day and had given me instead his gray flannel pants and blue woolen shirt. He was taller than I, so that I had to turn up the cuffs and sleeves, but it was the first time in almost three years that I had worn ordinary clothes, and I felt elegant, warm, and guilty.

By evening Karel's fever had gone up again; he was delirious and in pain, and my easier mood of the afternoon had subsided into weariness and despair.

Svestrom went through the camp files and came up with a bit of information I could have given him. He said, "Nussbaum in Four C is a doctor."

"He's a zombie."

"A zombie? What's that?"

"The living dead. People who the day the Gestapo picked them up said, 'God wills it so; I'm a dead man.' And except for the formality of dying, they are."

"I see. But I think we ought to try him. We can't just not do anything."

Dr. Nussbaum had been one of those who had let his hair and beard grow. Seeing him clean-shaven I realized for the first time that he was a young man, no older probably than the camp commander.

He kept well away from the bed, peered at Karel briefly and without interest, and diagnosed, "Typhus."

"We did not call you for a diagnosis, Dr. Nussbaum," said Svestrom. "We know it is typhus. What is the treatment?"

Nussbaum recited from some vague textbook memory: "Quinine, Antipyrrhin. Water or broth every hour. Chalk if there is diarrhea. Ice packs on the head. Don't move the patient."

"Morphine?" asked Svestrom.

For once Nussbaum was not vague. "Definitely not. Absolutely no morphine."

And there it was. Svestrom came and pulled me to my feet. "You must go to bed, Tyl. Yes. Because tomorrow you'll have to look after Karel while I try the hospitals in Linz and in Vienna, if I have to. One of them, somewhere, must have some quinine they can give us. So, have your dinner now and then go to sleep. I'll look after Killian."

I put my face against his hand, too tired and hopeless to try to speak. I thought I was too tired to eat, but once I started I found that I was starved, and remembered that I had not had anything but coffee since lunch the day before.

But I could not fall asleep. I was dressed more warmly than I had been since coming to the camp, yet I kept shivering and could not stop. After a while Svestrom looked in and said, "What's the matter, can't you get warm?" He went out and came back in a moment and put a jacket over my shoulders. I could tell by the feel of it that it was not one of his black tunics but the Afrika Korps jacket with the captain's badges on the shoulders.

I said, "Oh, no, don't," for this was still a uniform that had to be earned, the only one of the war, perhaps, that stood for something untarnished and entirely admirable.

"Why not? You have more right to it than I in any case. It doesn't belong to me. It was Gabriel's."

I might have guessed. The captain's badges, and the book of poems in the pocket. It would not require much imagination now, with the familiar jacket under his hand, in a dark room, to bend down and kiss Gabriel's mouth. I was too tired and defeated to resent it. But he only said, "Sleep now," and went back to Karel.

I put my face against the sleeve of Gabriel's jacket and felt the return of the sense of being looked after, of his kindness that had continued to work for me after he was dead.

My Elie grandmother used to believe that the dead take an active interest in the affairs of the living from the next world. I have no religion at all, and yet—Svestrom coming along to get me out of the quarry, another Pankow boy for Svestrom to sleep with—it was a Gabriel scheme all right. His presents had always had a ruthlessness about them, cutting through the frills of what one thought one ought to want to the heart's most secret desire.

The next day Karel was neither better nor worse, remaining delirious most of the day and famished only for water. Svestrom returned from Vienna without having accomplished much. "You'd think I was asking for truffles and champagne. I finally told them if they couldn't let me have any quinine I would be obliged to bring them all my typhus cases. That worked. I asked everyone for information because Nussbaum doesn't exactly inspire me with rocklike confidence, but I couldn't get two opinions that agreed. One doctor said cool baths to bring the fever down; the next one said absolutely not, moving the patient may be fatal. The one thing they all seem to agree on was: no morphine. It would be. The one thing we have enough of to kill a horse."

I said, "Well, anyway, whatever we do is as right as wrong. We can't be worse than the doctors."

I heated up the dinner they'd sent over earlier and we shared it, both of us too tired to be really hungry. Svestrom agreed to go to bed till midnight but made me promise to wake him then. The quinine seemed not to make much difference.

Karel remained the same for two weeks. In spite of all the water he drank he seemed dangerously dehydrated. Once or twice we thought his pulse had stopped, but we gave him brandy and he picked up a little. One doctor had said alcohol was fatal, but two others had recommended it for extreme weakness. It was terrifying, this constant guessing at remedies, never knowing whether they would cure or kill. I thought that, with all its pitfalls, it must be more restful to be an officer than a doctor.

On the thirteenth night of Karel's illness Svestrom shook me out of a dazed sleep to tell me that Karel was better. "He's been cursing for an hour at least."

I got up and went to the bedroom, where Karel, conscious and extremely disagreeable, complained of the bed, the nursing, and the food. Grubby beard, rash and all, I thought he was the most beautiful sight I'd ever seen, and if he hadn't had typhus I'd probably have kissed him.

I ran to the kitchen with orders from the camp commander for hot soup to be instantly produced, and while the cook got with it I shouted the good news in at the window of 4A.

Karel ate the soup and kept it down, growling, "Fuck off," at Marx, who had decided to share it with him. He slept through the next day without fever and by evening described the soup as miserable fucked-up slops and demanded a steak. Svestrom said, "Eat your soup. It's made from a bombed horse, not one that died of old age."

"Who bombs horses?"

"The Americans. They fly low and shoot at livestock. I imagine that is what they call 'severe losses inflicted on the civilian population' in their newscasts. It works out very well, in fact. They shoot them and I requisition them."

"They couldn't die in a better cause," said Karel and with a yawn went off to sleep again. He slept very quietly through the first part of the night, but when Svestrom took my place he was awake and talkative, and I could only hope he would behave himself, no longer having the excuse of delirium.

I was about to shut the door when I heard him say, "Why are you doing all this for me, General? What's one more dead prisoner in a place like this?"

I stayed where I was, leaving the door open a crack.

Svestrom said, "I am doing it because Tyl loves you and I love Tyl."

"Do you?" said Karel. "I didn't know. So do I. Though not quite the same way."

"Love is love," said Svestrom impatiently. "The rest is technicalities."

I could have laughed out loud, for Karel to meet finally

someone more arrogant than himself about technicalities and love.

"Tell me about it," said Svestrom. "Why do you love Tyl?"

"Because he wasn't down and out when he came here, I think. He was a mess—they'd worked him over at Mauthausen for some crack he made at one of the medical orderlies—but he was just mad, not cowed at all. He had another beating the next day because he couldn't remember his number. I'll bet he doesn't know it yet. He's spoiled and conceited and fucked-up politically, but nobody'll ever turn Tyl into prisoner number whatever it is. I don't like prisoners."

"I didn't like him at first," said Svestrom. "He has the three vices that are hardest to live with. He is dishonest, vain, and a snoop."

I was so furious I almost slammed the door.

"Those aren't vices," said Karel. "They're prison virtues. The tools of survival. I'm sort of disappointed in him right now. I've been teaching him how to survive for three years, and what does he do but nurse somebody with typhus. I don't think he'll ever get straightened out. Not really."

"Well, he has courage, loyalty, and generosity. They are the soldier's virtues. They don't make for survival. Would you say that the fact that he listens at doors is a tool for survival?"

"Does he?"

"Invariably."

"It's amazing how little information he gets for his troubles," said Karel.

"I'm sorry I've proved disappointing."

"I'll bet you are. Look, General, I'll probably croak anyway. Before I go, will you tell me something? What are you doing here?"

"Only what you see. Nothing interesting."

"What were you doing on July twentieth?"

"Curiosity about another person is a sign of recovery. Really sick people are only interested in themselves. Since you cannot guarantee that you will die, you will have to do without my secrets. I assure you you wouldn't find them worth dying for. Go to sleep. You too, Tyl. Good night."

The next morning Svestrom had another talk with Dr. Nussbaum, who said, "Fine, fine," but did not otherwise commit himself.

There were no more cases of typhus, and the people who worked at the munitions plant went back. Franticek came to the window and shouted that Operation Fuck-up was in full swing and we were winning the war. Fortunately Svestrom wasn't in at that particular moment.

Karel said, "I could do with a shave. Do you think you could manage without cutting my throat?"

I said, "Easily," not realizing until I actually set about it how difficult it is to shave another person, especially if that person fidgets and swears and gives a great deal of unhelpful advice. But it got done at last. Karel rubbed his hands across his chin and pronounced that I had done a rotten, fucked-up job.

After I'd cleaned up the mess we'd managed to make between us, I went back to sit with him. He said, "What are you wearing?"

"Some of Svestrom's things. He lent them to me. We had to boil all our things, you know."

"They can't be boiling for two weeks."

Svestrom had never mentioned my uniform and neither had I. It was so pleasant to be wearing clothes like a human being again that I was reluctant to do anything about it. Yet I felt guilty, for I was not a human being; I was a prisoner, and the pretense was a disloyalty to our side.

To Karel I said, "Don't introduce disgusting diseases into the camp and we can all go back to wearing our rightful clothes," and seeing his scowl, could not help adding, "Karel, Karel, I'm so damned glad."

"Well, don't get all worked up yet. I may still have to fuck off."

"Are you feeling worse?"

"Not very. I'm all right. But I've seen typhus before and this happens a lot of times. You get better, and then you either get well or else you get worse again and croak. We'll see. I don't care either way."

"Karel, you're a survivor." I began to be afraid again. It wasn't like Karel not to care whether he lived or died. And his color was bad.

"Yeah. Listen, Tyl, I want to talk to you. About Svestrom. He's a problem for you, isn't he?"

"He's been one for quite a while."

"I don't mean that. If you aren't used to that yet just resign yourself. It won't last all that much longer."

"He's been very decent to you, Karel."

"I know. He is very decent. I mean, so he's a fairy, though you wouldn't think it to look at him, really, but hell, I mean, everybody doesn't have to like the same thing. I mean, cats like mice; I don't, see. So that's not in it at all."

"What is, then?"

"The other thing he is: the Nazi general. The camp. Why we're here. Other camps, much worse ones. Colonel Shit, the things he used to do. Being free to do them with nobody to stop him. You see, Tyl, that's what you have to remember. People like Svestrom make people like Colonel Shit possible. So they're worse because they're better. Do you follow me? He makes it difficult for people to remember, but he remembers it all right. It doesn't seem fair in a way that it's the decent ones that punish themselves the most, but in another way it is fair. They're the ones who should have known better."

"People make honest mistakes, Karel."

"Sure. But who says you don't get punished for an honest mistake? Look, you walk in front of a bus because you didn't see it; that's an honest mistake. But you end up just as dead as the man who walked in front of it to commit suicide.

"Anyway, it's not Svestrom I'm worried about. It's you. You like him, don't you?"

"Yes, Karel."

"I know. It's all right, Tyl. He's a hard man to dislike. But the thing you've got to remember is what side he's on. Colonel Shit's side, Himmler's side, Auschwitz's side. You have to remember it when it's hardest to do, when you like him the most, when he's at his best. If you forget, if you reach across, you betray us. All the ones who are dead and can't fight back any more."

He looked gray and tired. I didn't want to argue with him, but there was one thing I had to say. "He saved your life, Karel."

His mouth went down in his old, derisive smile. "Fuck off. I know who saved my life. I wasn't as far out of my head as all that."

"Stop talking, Karel. You're making yourself tired."

He was silent, his head turned from the window. "Can you draw the curtain, Tyl? It's too bright in here."

I got up and drew the blackout curtains across the windows. It was a day of black skies and drenching rain. I went back to the bed. Karel put out his hand and I took it in mine. "Sleep a bit. You're tired."

He moved fretfully and shut his eyes. His mouth was tight with the pain he would not admit to, and his hand was clenched on mine. We had been like this many times, nights after the quarry: his hand the only hold I had on sanity. He was not a life line now.

By afternoon Karel was hemorrhaging and in terrible pain. Svestrom sent for Dr. Nussbaum, who stood at a safe distance and gave it as his opinion that Karel was hemorrhaging, that there was nothing we could do, and that morphine was definitely not to be given.

Svestrom did not suggest taking my place so I could sleep. No one could sleep through this. He stayed with me, across the bed from me, the ruined side of his face turned to me. Finally he said, "It doesn't make sense. They give morphine to stop bleeding. I know they do in the field hospitals. It can't be wrong to give it for hemorrhaging."

I'd given in long ago. I said, "Dear God, Johannes, I don't care if it is wrong. We've got to take the chance. Give it to him."

"Yes. I will."

He went to the bathroom and unlocked the cabinet. He handed me the hypodermic. "Do you know how to do this? You're probably less clumsy than I."

My hands were numb with Karel's hold on them, but I took the hypodermic. I wanted to be the one to do it. When I had filled the syringe, Svestrom held out his good hand and said, "Let me."

"No. He's *my* friend."

Karel was so thin, yet it was difficult to find a vein. Being a doctor's son gives one no inherited talent for this sort of thing.

It worked quickly, at least. In the moment between the easement of pain and the drowsiness of the drug, Karel's eyes recognized me. "Thanks." The eyes wandered, came back. "Tyl, remember. What we talked about."

"Yes, Karel."

"Promise."

"Of course I promise."

He allowed the drug to take over then, growing incoherent and finally falling asleep. Svestrom said, "None of the doctors said anything about this."

"Karel knew."

He was silent for a long time. Then he said, "Tyl, it was an overdose."

"Yes." He had put murder on his conscience so that my friend could die without pain. "Yes," I lied. "I knew it."

10 ━━━━━━━━━━━━━━━━━━━━━━━━━━━━

The frost which had begun the night of Karel's illness had held. It probably saved us; for the moment there were no more cases of typhus. But the ground was frozen solid and Svestrom said, "How will we ever dig a grave?"

"There are pickaxes in the quarry. Don't you remember?"

"Of course. Tyl, let the Reds dig the grave. They haven't been able to do anything for Karel until now. It's not their fault, but I imagine it must bother them. They can have that, at least."

Franticek and Paul came to the window, and I told them what to do. They dug the grave at the edge of the river by the barbed-wire fence and carried Karel down, wrapped in the blanket in which we had first carried him to the camp commander's house. The rabbi told Franticek the blanket should have been boiled in carbolic and saved for the living. Karel would have approved of this because he was a survivor. Franticek bloodied the rabbi's nose, and Karel was buried in the airforce-blue shroud with *Flugstaffel 117–7* stamped in the corner.

I stayed with Svestrom, watching from the window of the camp commander's house. We couldn't be sure we hadn't caught Karel's typhus, and it was better not to come near the others. We had no service for him, for we were all loyal atheists. It crossed my mind that it was as well there were no eulogies for Karel, who had been revolutionary, mother hen, pimp, hero, schoolmaster, murderer, friend.

Nor were there tears. While the Reds were shoveling the frozen dirt back into the grave, the first swan of the spring came sailing down our stream. The swans lived on a pond in the village, Jacques had once told me. And sometimes they floated past the camp, beautiful and free, not deigning to turn their heads toward the prison.

The gravediggers flung down their shovels and tore through the barbed wire before I could run down to help them.

"What are they doing?" asked Svestrom. "Not escaping, I hope. It's still very cold at night."

A tussle of arms, legs, white wings slashing the air, an outraged honk, and at last a white neck drooping with a fluted limpness which would have been the envy of Pavlova.

"He's for their dinner," I told Svestrom. "What do you suppose swans taste like?"

It was one hell of a funeral.

Abri brought us a piece of the swan that night. "For you and the general," he said. I understood. It would have been normal to share it with me. That they offered part of it to Svestrom meant no relenting, but their thank-you for taking care of Karel.

Swans taste fishy and are tougher than horse meat.

For the last time Svestrom sent for Dr. Nussbaum. He asked, "What is the incubation period for typhus?"

"What?"

"How long before we can be sure we did not catch it? Pankow ought not to return to the barracks before we can be certain there will be no contagion."

Nussbaum said, "Two weeks."

"Thank you. You can go."

I have no idea what the incubation period for typhus is. Neither, I am sure, had Nussbaum. He merely did not wish to be left without an answer. He might with as much assurance have said two days or two months.

As arbitrarily I accepted these two weeks as Karel's gift to me: permission to have two weeks outside time, away from the opposing camps, spent on the forbidden middle ground. I did not forget that two weeks are only fourteen days and would pass; I knew I must not make any commitments which would outlast a breath, but that was the only discipline I imposed on myself. For all the rest I put away my defenses and accepted Svestrom as father, friend, lover, and beloved.

I wish I had kept a journal of those two weeks. Nothing elaborate, just a cipher for each day, a word—snowdrops, suicide, time, love, typhus, Gabriel—which would release the memory of each day. I think I have kept them all, but memory modifies and amends. I have tried to keep everything as it was, for those two weeks are all I shall ever have of him. For the sake of those two weeks I cannot regret anything. Not Karel's death (I have said it at last), not the time that led up to them at Heiligendorf, nor all the months since: the sleepless prowling nights and the strangers.

It seems odd now, but I don't think in those two weeks I worried once whether I had caught Karel's typhus, and neither, I believe, did Svestrom. The food we ate, rotten potatoes and watery cabbage, sawdust bread and turnips, kept us in a constant state of bellyaches anyway. Under normal circumstances I imagine I would have spent many hours in front of the mirror checking my tongue for patches, watching for headache and fever, and imagining symptoms.

But my days were full of other occupations. Waiting for footsteps up the walk to the house, the sound of the door latch, the pleased breath that always came before his, "Hello, Tyl." It's not much of a name, Tyl, one inflexible syllable. Johannes is better, a kiss on the tongue, three syllables like the *I love you* which I might not say because it is a commitment that outlasts two weeks.

Sharing the wretched meals with pleasure, locking the door and listening to the BBC turned low to suppress the embarrassing giveaway notes of Beethoven's *Fifth,* making no comment on the end of a world, Berlin burning, Dresden leveled to the ground, four armies closing in upon us, ashamed to witness these events and have only one thought: What of us? After all this is over, what will become of us two?

His hard, ruined body against mine at last, the blind encounter, racing heart and violated breath, teeth and fists clenched on time, failing always in the endeavor to impose permanence, but gaining from violence a distillate of joy and a nearness so close that I could not have said whose breath filled my mouth, his or mine.

Time hounds like furies at such moments. Conscious of the ticking of his watch at my shoulder, I closed my hand on it, as he many times closed his over the number on my wrist in the act of love.

"What is it?"

"I don't like to hear the time passing."

He opened the watch strap and dropped his watch on the floor. "It has stopped."

The snow began to melt once more the day after Karel's funeral. The ground turned to mud, icicles dripped, the air was filled with the sound of rushing water under a washed April sun. I saw Svestrom walk across the river meadow and stoop for something in the wet, snow-patched grass. When he came in he held out his hand. "Tyl, look. Snowdrops. The first this year."

I said, "My first spring here all the snow melted off the river meadow one afternoon. It was an awful winter—the Stalingrad winter—and a lot of people died of starvation and cold. When all the snow had melted, with not even a patch of white left, we really felt for the first time that we'd survived. The next morning, when we got up, we saw the meadow was white again. I was so miserable I wanted to die. And Karel said, "Don't pay any attention, Tyl. It's nothing but a lot of fucking snowdrops.""

Svestrom said, "Once, in Berlin, Gabriel bought a whole flower stall of sunflowers because he liked the way they looked. They took up so much space we had to rent another room just for them. These are for you."

"Could we give them to Karel, Johannes?" It bothered me, that untended, unmarked grave.

"Of course."

We found an egg cup in the kitchen. I hadn't seen an egg for so long, the cup looked to me like some ancient cooking implement in a museum. I put the snowdrops into it and carried them down to the grave. Franticek came down and said everybody sent me regards, and wasn't it kind of grim, being stuck for two solid weeks in the camp commander's house?

"It's not bad."

"He scares me."

"Franti, what shit. Why?"

"I don't know. He's just sort of formidable, you know."

"He's all right."

"Oh, well," said Franticek, "it's only two weeks. It won't last forever."

We had two more cases of typhus after the warm weather started. They were in 4C and were treated in the customary camp manner. I did not tell Svestrom about it. There was nothing to be done.

We could hear them, though, that night. Svestrom said, "What is that?"

I explained.

He said, "They can't be left out there."

"It's better that way."

"Tyl!"

"How much morphine have you got left?"

"None."

I knew it. He had given the rest to Nussbaum for a boy in 4C who had been careless at the munitions factory and had blown his hand off.

"Look, Johannes, it's a cold night, they're delirious now, and they'll be dead by morning. Is it really kinder to let them go on for two weeks and die like Karel, without any morphine to make it easier?"

He turned away to pace the room while I remained by the open window. Once he stopped his pacing to put his uniform tunic across my shoulders, then went back and forth again, the sound of his limp noticeable in the still room.

I put my hands to my shoulders, touching the silver and gold braid, thinking, This is what it's like to be inside that uniform. You put it on and you have absolute power. You decide who lives and dies, you can be just or arbitrary, kind or sadistic, and no one can stop you as long as you wear that uniform. I began to understand Colonel Shit.

He stopped behind me suddenly and slammed the window shut. "What is it, Tyl?"

"I was thinking what it's like to be inside this uniform."

He made a smothered sound of protest and his good arm went around my shoulders and the black cloth so hard that it hurt. With his mouth against my hair he said, scarcely audible, "Oh, my Tyl. With all that's happened to you I'll always be grateful that that's one thing you'll never have to know: what it's like inside that uniform."

He took the tunic from my shoulder and handed me his leather coat instead.

"Put this on. I've had an idea. You'll have to give me a hand. I can't manage it alone."

"Give you a hand to what?"

"Bring two blankets."

I followed him down to the edge of the grass where the two sick men were. We got them into the blankets and carried them to the Mercedes. They were delirious and did not protest. They weren't any help either.

Svestrom got into the driver's seat while I was still pointing out to him that no hospital anywhere would take two Jews with typhus. "I know," he said. "Go back to bed, Tyl," and started the car. For a little I could follow the lights on the winding road, but they had by law to be covered with black paper with only a narrow slit cut into it, and I soon lost them. There was only the noise of the old muffler. Sounds are deceptive at night in the mountains, or I would have sworn he was driving past the village, not down to Linz but uphill.

I went inside and straightened the sheets on the bed. Paranoiac neatness had never prevailed against love's disorder. Our blankets were in the car. I was cold. I covered myself with his leather coat. It was warm and it was his.

"You will never have to know what it is like inside that uniform."

A prison of well-tailored black broadcloth, with the general's silver and gold epaulettes. The prison of a mutilated body within the prison of the uniform within the prison of Heiligendorf. All life a prison, hate a prison, and love even more so—with which philosophic reflection I fell asleep.

When I woke again Svestrom was back. He'd made himself a pot of tea.

"Sevensleeper. Do you want some tea?"

"Please. Where did you go, Johannes?"

"Up to the convent. It suddenly occurred to me that the nuns are the very people to take care of our sick. I was thinking of it on religious grounds, but it turns out that I was more right than I knew. Most of them are nurses. They used to be a missionary order. I wish I'd thought of it sooner. They would have been able to look after Killian a lot better than we."

The picture of Karel being nursed by nuns in a convent made me choke into my tea. "Poor Karel. It was bad enough being taken care of by a—a—"

"A Nazi general?"

"What did the Mother Superior say? I'm surprised she didn't throw you into a ravine."

"I think she would be quite capable of it. I wonder why we always think of nuns as meek. This one is a termagant. Fortunately she didn't mind taking the typhus cases."

"I'll bet."

"No, really. She said she'd long been exercised about the camp and wondered how she could help. Their own position is so precarious that she hadn't felt free to make advances to us, but she said if I ordered her to take care of my sick people she would of course have to obey. So I ordered her to and that was that."

"You look awfully pleased with yourself."

"I am. It's like having a private hospital for the camp."

"Those two men will probably die anyway."

"Probably. But at least they won't die in a damp meadow on a cold night."

"On the other hand the nuns may get typhus and die too."

"On the other hand the two men may get well with competent nursing and none of the nuns may get it. I'll be damned if I accept the responsibility of playing God, Tyl."

"It's like the fliers."

"What is?"

"Do you think they were spies, Johannes?"

"I don't know. I imagine so. I know the Americans have an organization whose members go behind enemy lines in uniform in the hope that if they get caught they'll be treated as prisoners of war. Perhaps the English do too. On the other hand, if they were spies they would have had cyanide."

"They did."

"Then I think you can safely assume that they were not fliers."

"If they'd admitted that to Colonel Shit he might have killed them or not, I don't know. But that was their lookout. By keeping quiet, which was obviously their duty, they were responsible for an innocent person being killed."

"You never told me that part."

So I told him about Blitzstein, who had died badly and alone, surrendered to power by those who should have been his protection.

"One could argue that the responsibility was Colonel Weizeck's."

"It was theirs too."

"It's very complicated. But then stupidity always complicates things."

"Why stupidity?"

"Look at it, Tyl. This whole business about the fliers was fantastically stupid. On their part, to be behind the lines in the uniform of an enemy country; on our part that Weizeck was ever made a colonel and put in charge of anything more responsible than a pig farm—one could probably go on a good long time to the stupidities that create concentration camps and Weizecks in the first place. Tell me, how do you happen to know about the cyanide?"

"John gave some to Karel."

He looked startled. "Where is it now?"

"I really couldn't tell you. The last I knew it was in Colonel Shit's coffee."

"I see."

"I couldn't tell you while Karel was alive."

"There was a suicide note, wasn't there?"

"Yes. Peter forged that. Nobody investigated very closely. I suppose it was a good time for suicides."

He said, "Yes, indeed. Did no one suggest that the obvious manner of suicide for an officer is to shoot himself?"

"Not anyone who knew Colonel Shit."

"No, probably not. Why did the fliers not use the cyanide? It's certainly quicker and easier than hanging."

"I suppose they would have if Shit had decided to hang them all at the same time. But with picking one and then another and no one knowing whether he'd go on or stop, the one who took the cyanide would just have given the show away for the rest."

"It was very brave of them, but what an odd people they are, the English. Had they been German officers they would have all taken their cyanide together and spared everyone a lot of fuss."

On April 19, the senior guard, Sergeant Steiger, came in the evening to inform General von Svestrom that of all the glorious holidays of the Third Reich, Camp Heiligendorf had always celebrated the Führer's birthday especially, since without this birthday there would of course have been no Third Reich.

Svestrom listened with a straight face but began to frown when Sergeant Steiger said that Camp Heiligendorf had always begun the Glorious Birthday with an oration by the camp commander, and that he was sure the *Herr General* would wish to continue this fine tradition.

He had tried this kind of arm-twisting on Svestrom before, but never with less success than now.

"I think it's an excellent idea to remember the Führer's birthday," said Svestrom. "I won't make a speech, but we'll give everybody double rations, sergeant."

Sergeant Steiger said, "Yes, sir." There really wasn't anything else he could say, but I didn't like the look on his face.

We listened to the BBC news. It was not as cheerful as the Führer might have wished for his birthday, the Russians having arrived in Berlin.

After we'd gone to bed that night I said, "I don't think Sergeant Steiger approves of you, Johannes."

"That's all right. I don't approve of him either."

"Could he make trouble for you?"

"I can't imagine how."

"He's got a lot of connections in Linz."

"I don't really see what he could do."

"What were you doing on July twentieth?" The question surprised me more than it did him. It must have been at the back of my mind since Karel had asked it.

"I was delivering a report from Rommel to Hitler's headquarters in Rastenburg."

"Is that where it happened?"

"I suppose the proper answer to that is 'what?' But, yes, that was where it happened. Though my being there was accidental. Keitel had been telling Hitler that we were holding the Allies in Normandy, and it was simply not true. I was there to tell him so. I didn't know they were going to plant the bomb that day. They'd tried so many times before and failed. It was what Karel would have called a thoroughly fucked-up operation. If I were to tell you all the attempts that were made and failed I would have to talk like Scheherazade, and you're not going to stay with me one thousand and one nights, are you, Tyl?"

I shook my head against his shoulder. It seemed an unfair question to taunt me with.

"No," he said. "I know. I expect some day when the tragedy has worn off and all the people concerned in it are dead, some of those stories are going to seem like pure comedy. Once, in the early days, Hitler flew to Russia to inspect the front. On the way back General von Tresckow gave Colonel Brandt, who was on the same plane, a bomb done up as a parcel, saying it was a gift of brandy for General Stieff and asking him to deliver it. Unfortunately the bomb didn't explode. You can imagine the lame excuses everyone had to invent to get their 'brandy' back. Things like that were forever happening. People put bombs in their overcoat pockets at parades, planning to jump on Hitler, only the bombs failed to explode or Hitler was late or the parade was canceled."

"I'd no idea it went on so long."

"Oh, yes. I wasn't in on it at the beginning. I was in Africa enjoying the war, I was in love, who had time to think? Please don't think I say that as an excuse. There's no excuse for not thinking, ever. We're all paying for it now, and rightly so.

"Then, after Gabriel was killed, I spent about a year in that ambivalent frame of mind where I was determined not to kill myself but didn't see why the English shouldn't do it for me. All I got for my pains was a collection of medals. Finally, at Kasserine Pass, I had my leg shot to bits, and when I got out of the hospital they gave me a staff job in Berlin while I got used to walking again. Funny. If it hadn't been for that I'd be a prisoner of war in Egypt now."

I rolled him a cigarette and lit it for him. "Go on, Johannes. Please."

"Well, Berlin was where it all really started for me. The town was full of people I'd known all my life: cousins, friends, people I'd been to school with. And every one of them was busy trying to murder Hitler.

"My orderly used to say the conspiracy consisted entirely of cousins, godfathers of each other's children and witnesses at each others' weddings. It was a fair description. The only person I think who was a stranger to me was Klaus von Stauffenberg—"

"An unspeakably vile murder attempt was today carried out by a Colonel von Stauffenberg—"

"Yes, that one. He came from southern Germany somewhere, Bamberg, I think. Though as it turned out his mother was related to the Gneisenaus, so we were umpteenth cousins of some sort. What was that you said, the unspeakably vile murder thing?"

"That was Goebbels's speech that night. It followed right after Hitler's. Didn't you hear it?"

"No. I suppose when it becomes possible to write the history of that day, he will be just that: the person who placed the bomb. That always seems to happen to people who achieve fame or notoriety through one single act. The act becomes the person. It will happen to Stauffenberg, too. It's a pity. He deserves better than that."

"What happened to him, afterwards?"

"I was told he was shot that night. If it is true he was luckier than most of his colleagues. I hope it's true. I didn't know him well, but I liked him.

"I wasn't in Berlin for long, you know. When Rommel was sent to command the troops in France he asked me to be his chief of staff. Dear God, the army in France! What a shock after the Afrika Korps. New recruits, badly trained or not trained at all. Not enough weapons, no morale whatever. After D Day it was just butchery. It made the fighting in Africa look like a tournament, prestigious, but entirely unreal.

"Everyone always seems to assume the Afrika Korps was hand-picked. That isn't true. They were just tank corps soldiers with desert warfare training. The rest was due to Rommel, in part, and to the desert, somehow. There's a special dash to desert fighting. I suspect if you don't have it or acquire it fast you don't last long enough to leave a mark.

"France was a charnel house. We knew from the first day we hadn't a chance. But our orders were directly from the OKW. Stand and fight. The report Rommel asked me to take to Rastenburg must have been the hundred and ninety-ninth to explain why we couldn't.

"Stauffenberg nearly dropped the bomb when he saw me there. He managed to warn me, not that I needed it. It had gotten so that whenever anyone saw Stauffenberg with a briefcase they ran for cover. He said he was going to take a phone call, and I had better go to the lavatory. People really weren't supposed to leave the room at all while Hitler was there.

"Stauffenberg put his briefcase down next to Hitler. On the other side of the briefcase was good old Colonel Brandt; you remember, the one with the brandy bottles. I was just on the point of vanishing unobtrusively out the door when I saw him pick up Stauffenberg's briefcase and move it to the other side of the table leg. I suppose it was in his way. It wouldn't have mattered with an ordinary table, but this particular map table was supported on heavy posts, quite heavy enough to deflect the blast of a bomb. The only thing to be done was to move the briefcase back to the other side again.

"I didn't know how much time there was left. A minute or two, at most. I crept around peoples' backs, looking harmless. I had to reach around Brandt, and it saved my life, I suppose. I don't really know. The next thing I knew I was in the Rastenburg hospital, feeling like hell and in no shape whatever to listen to Goebbels make speeches, I assure you. Brandt was killed, of course.

"The doctor at the hospital, the one you're always so unkind about, turned out to be an old acquaintance from the Afrika Korps. Most of the things that happened afterwards I learned from him. Of course everyone who was even remotely suspected of being connected with the plot was arrested. I couldn't imagine why no one came for me. I didn't find out till much later that I owed it all to Keitel, who, I regret to say, is an old friend of my father's. But it wasn't that. It was simply that he'd seen me move toward the briefcase, and so he theorized that I couldn't possibly have known there was a bomb in it or I would have been on my way out the door. The Gestapo didn't believe a word of it, but Keitel is too high up to be contradicted. So they gave me Heiligendorf. I'm sure they expected me to shoot myself rather than accept it. It was the obvious solution for them. They were in the clear as far as Keitel was concerned, and they would have my corpse as well."

"Only you didn't shoot yourself."

"You think I should have, Tyl?"

"Yes."

"So did I. I started to clean my gun—a clumsy, one-handed, one-eyed job it was; it seemed to take forever—when my doctor came into the room. I didn't even bother to make up a story, it seemed such an obvious course to take. I'd not realized that a doctor thinks of every situation in terms of saving lives rather than honor. He brought up the side of the problem I had not given a moment's thought to: your side. He pointed out that to two hundred people at Heiligendorf it was a matter of life and death whether I or some SS bastard ran the place. I said that was your problem. Mine was much simpler. Svestroms don't run concentration camps. My doctor friend got quite annoyed with me. He took my gun away. He said he would give it back in the morning if I hadn't changed my mind by then. He wanted me to spend the night thinking it over. He had my gun, so I agreed, though I couldn't see anything to think over.

"But in the course of the night I remembered something Gabriel had once said, as a toast, when he was drunk. 'May we never die in a good cause.' I remember scolding him. Tank corps people are as superstitious as sailors, and they don't like toasts about dying. Gabriel said it was his theory that good causes were only the itch of someone's bad conscience and that they tend to be at best uncomfortable, at worst deadly to a great many people who have no interest in them at all. You know, the Crusades, the Inquisition, religious wars, things like that. Gabriel had said he wanted no part of it, and I had agreed with him. It now occurred to me that our plot to kill Hitler was a perfect example of what Gabriel had been talking about. Our conscience had itched—very late in the day, in some cases, including my own—and the result was I don't know how many dead. Hundreds, certainly. Perhaps more. Many of them not even connected with the plot or only connected by being relatives; wives, parents, children.

"Being a survivor is hard on the conscience anyhow. One feels the need of an excuse for still being alive. I used the two hundred people at Heiligendorf as my excuse."

I had no answer to that.

He said, "You think I did the wrong thing, don't you, Tyl?"

"It got me out of the quarry."

"But you think it was wrong."

"We'd never have survived last winter under Colonel Shit."

"But it was the wrong thing."

"Yes."

"I think so too. One has all the facts and they lie like Ananias."

Svestrom's revolver in its leather holster was slung across the back of a chair. The circling searchlight picked out the dull gleam of the leather. I had to ask it at last.

"After you were done here, Johannes, after the Russians got here, you were going to shoot yourself."

He said idly, "Don't be melodramatic."

"Am I?"

"Even if I was, Tyl, I shan't now."

I doubt that I would have had the courage to speak of it had I not known that too. "What changed your mind?"

"Don't be coy."

"I'm not coy. You won't have me much longer."

"Dear God, your vanity is really fantastic. It has absolutely nothing to do with having or not having you. Only with loving you at a time and in a place where I thought I had come in the most literal sense of the word to a dead end."

"You had me when you went to Rommel's funeral. You thought they'd pick you up there, didn't you?"

"I didn't love you then. I didn't even like you."

"You had a funny way of showing it."

"Because I went to bed with you? Oh, Tyl! You were a spoiled self-pitying brat with Gabriel's face. You'd told me how the camp—and you—felt on the subject. I was drunk. I'm not making excuses. It's never excusable to take advantage of a person who's not in a position to defend himself. But I don't consider it one of the major crimes of history, and I can't, now, honestly say I'm sorry."

"When did you change your mind about my being a spoiled brat?"

"Never. It is possible to fall in love with a brat, you know. And I don't think one ever begins by liking a person one is going to fall in love with. Liking makes for friendship."

"But what made you fall in love all of a sudden? It seems so peculiar."

"It wasn't sudden and it wasn't any one thing. The fact that you were always forgetting to be afraid of me, more than anything else, I think. Taking my side against the fliers the day after Rommel's funeral. Bringing me a present for Christmas."

Marx, with the ability of cats to recognize that they are being talked about, no matter how indirectly, uncurled himself, found a new position, set up a rumbling purr, and went back to sleep.

Svestrom said, "I've given you a present now. You realize, don't you, that you now have it in your power to kill me?"

"Oh, thanks very much. It's just what I always wanted."

"You don't believe me? You think no one would take your word against mine? I'm a very suspect person, Tyl. The smallest thing, as small as the word of a boy in a concentration camp, could push me over the line."

"Who's being melodramatic now?"

"Tell Sergeant Steiger and see what happens."

"Is that what you want?"

"No, of course not. Nobody wants to be strangled with piano wire."

"Then why did you tell me?"

"Because I want you to know. Because if I have the power of life and death over you I want you to have it over me. Because I don't believe love is possible except between equals. I love you, Tyl. I love you. And I terribly want you to love me."

No ghost fingered the window or rattled the door latch. When I moved there was a whiff of carbolic from the blanket. In this house Karel had died. "If you reach out you betray us." I said nothing.

From the office of Reichsführer Heinrich Himmler to Major General Johannes Quentin von Svestrom, directive number something-or-other subsection blah blah to arrange for immediate transfer of the inmates of Camp Heiligendorf to Dachau in order to effect with all speed the final blah blah.

I found it crumpled in the wastepaper basket and smoothed it out from habit rather than curiosity. I don't remember being frightened, but I must have been because I had to sit down on the bed. My knees had gone soft. After all this time!

Svestrom found me, still sitting, still with directive whatever-it-was in my hand. It didn't disturb him that I had been reading his mail. It wasn't the first time, and he never had private letters anyway.

I said, "What will you do?"

"Nothing. Nothing at all. Just put it back in the wastebasket."

He sat down beside me. He had the drawn look of being in pain and desperately tired. I had slept most of the night, but I could tell from the number of cigarette ends in the ash tray by the bed that he had not.

"But, Johannes—"

"Tyl, nobody in this camp is going to Dachau. That's final."

"What if they send soldiers?"

"Just like that? You don't know army red tape, my dear. First they'll send follow-up directive so-and-so, then follow-up query something-else to follow up the follow-up directive. Then they'll possibly send a messenger to find out what the devil is going on. None of this happens overnight. I have very little doubt that I can stall them till the Russians get here. If I can't I'll just have to let you all go free a bit sooner. You can hide in the woods till the Russians arrive. I don't want to do that, though, except as a last resort, because a lot of the prisoners aren't in very good shape and would probably catch pneumonia. Here they have at least a roof over their heads."

It sounded reasonable, but I was still afraid. I realized that my fear, from the first, had not been for myself. I'd known he would look after us.

"Johannes, if we clear out, what will you do?"

"Invent some terribly lame excuses, I imagine."

"I don't think that's funny."

"No," he said agreeably.

"What do you think they'll do to you when they find you with an empty camp?"

"I don't know, Tyl. Shoot me, hang me, scold me, nothing. None of it will happen." He took the paper from my fingers, crumpled it up again, and threw it back in the wastebasket. Then he stretched out on the bed, his head on my knees. "You don't realize how confused everything is outside. The railroads are fouled up and haven't any coal anyway; the roads are full of bomb craters. Even if I sent you to Dachau today I doubt that you'd get there in time. I'm damned tired, Tyl. I wish you could teach me to sleep."

"My one talent."

"Not entirely."

His hair slid through my fingers: nice hair, straight and fine and always very clean. Not like mine, which is the texture as well as the color of straw.

"Funny, it coming like that," he said. "If we survive I must tell my doctor friend. He will be pleased. I never expected him to be proved right in such a definite, recognizable way. I thought it would be just scrounging food and blankets *ad nauseam*."

"Does it make you feel better?"

"Of course. Not any more in the right, though."

I was still not reassured, but he looked too tired to be badgered with questions. Like most bad sleepers he was often able to sleep for an hour or two at unplanned times during the day. And, like all lovers of insomniacs, I had become expert at recognizing such times.

I took my hand from his hair. He shook his head. "Don't stop. I like it."

"I like it too. You have nice hair." Trivial talk was usually better than silence for trapping him into sleep. "When I first saw you, at the quarry, I thought it was the same color as mine."

"It used to be, almost."

"When did it go white?"

He smiled. "You want me to tell you something romantic, don't you? Like the day Gabriel died. As a matter of fact it happened years ago. It seems to be a family trait. My mother was completely white by the time she was twenty-five. Or so I am told. For as long as I can remember she's been every color but white."

"I like it white."

"I rather do myself."

Belatedly I realized the obvious. "Karin von Svestrom is your mother."

"Of course. Who did you think she was?"

"Your wife, as a matter of fact."

I think he'd been half asleep. Now he sat up, half laughing, half annoyed. "Really, Tyl, you of all people might have noticed that I am not a marrying man."

"People don't only marry for sex," I said, feeling a prize fool.

"Really? Do tell."

"They might need an heir."

"True. Fortunately I had an older brother who did all the right things. He went to sea, married an heiress, had three sons, commanded a U-boat, and died a hero. My mother would have preferred it if I had been the dead hero, but she can't have everything her way, though a long life of disappointments hasn't disabused her of the idea."

"Why don't you like your mother?"

"Because she's not a likable person."

"Did you like your brother?"

"Yes, surprisingly I did. He was such a boy scout, so proper, so damned nice about it, he made me laugh."

"If your brother hadn't supplied the heirs, would you have?"

"I suppose I could have tried."

"Haven't you ever, at all?"

"No. The temptation has been nonexistent."

"Gabriel used to."

"Yes, I know. You will too."

It seemed very remote. "Will I?"

"Why not? You mustn't attach too much importance to this. The circumstances are peculiar, after all. And in any case one affair with a queer doesn't make you homosexual any more than a sunburn makes you a Negro."

I remembered how jealous I had once been of the Baronin von Svestrom and began to laugh.

"What?"

"Karin von Svestrom. I used to hate her guts."

He stretched out again, sleepy and gentle. He had the gift of the present. Tomorrow might be pain, Dachau, the noose, or love again. He would deal with it when it came. I could never learn from him. I had always to prod ant heaps, bite nails, pick scabs. He said, "I like it when you're jealous. I've only been in love three times in my life. With my housemaster at school, with Gabriel, and with you."

I was not sleepy and not gentle. Prodder and scab picker, I said, "I am Gabriel."

He smiled, half asleep. "It's very presumptuous of you, my dear, to think there could ever be the slightest confusion."

The night is almost over. Orion's sword has slid under the window frame. I can hear a guard passing outside on his rounds of the camp. It is Haber. I know all their footsteps apart. Haber walks easier now that Karel is dead.

You're not asleep, Johannes, for all you lie so quietly. I know your eyes are open in the dark.

Any other night I could have slept, my head on your arm. But this night is our last, and now it is almost over.

There will be other nights, one week, perhaps two if the Russians take their time. But this is the last all the same. Our two weeks of quarantine are over. It was quarantine from a lot of things that had nothing to do with typhus, our holiday in no man's land. It was the bargain that two weeks would be all the time we would have like this. It's the bargain that we now go back to what we were, and that in a week or two we won't even have that.

But how can we go back, Johannes? You have left us no fences. Not even that of prisoner—jailer. What else was there left between us?

Johannes, Johannes. Your name is my code word for love. How will I ever call you "sir" again?

"Please, sir, can I have my uniform?"

"Of course, Tyl."

It was clean and smelled of carbolic. My body had forgotten how demeaning it was. But it was mine. The gray flannels and woolen blue shirt were not.

He waited till I had changed and hung away his things, so that he was speaking to the prisoner.

"Don't go for a moment yet, Tyl. There's something I want to say to you. This is the end of your job here. From now on, if you come, it will be because you choose to, not because I ordered you to. If you choose to stay away I will not send for you."

My mind was dazed with the pain of the all-or-nothing gamble he was taking because I knew what he did not: that it was the end between us.

He said, "Do you love me, Tyl?"

Through the window I could see Karel's grave and in the room I could feel, for the first time in fourteen days, his presence. Alone I could not have kept silent.

He said, "I thought sometimes, these last weeks—" and touched his face with weary disgust. "Of course not, how could you?"

This familiar gesture at last wrenched the truth from me. "I do. I love you."

Karel said, "I'll never forgive you for this through all eternity."

Svestrom's hand closed hard on my shoulder. "What's the matter, Tyl? What's wrong?"

Karel said, "Tell him."

I said, "You are a Nazi general."

"Yes."

"Go on," said Karel. "Finish."

"You're my enemy."

"No."

"Look at your uniform and look at mine."

"We aren't always in uniform. There has been an armistice, Tyl."

"That's cheating."

He smiled. "I suppose it is. So what does it come to? That you love Johannes and hate General von Svestrom?"

"No. It's much worse than that. You don't have to split yourself in two for me. I loved General von Svestrom before I knew Johannes."

"Tyl!" His face had the drawn punished look I had not seen since the day John had told him about the meathooks.

"I've been cheating you a long time, Johannes. You know there's no such thing as an armistice. My side is at war with yours, and I was as much under oath to them as you were to your army. Now I've betrayed them. Dead people who can't fight back."

"Yes, I suppose you have. But you haven't cheated me. I told you about that."

Ruinously I remembered, not, "It has nothing to do with having or not having you," but, "Look at me, who do you think would have me for love now?" and my silence in reply. As if touched by the same recollection, he put his hand to his face with the weary, disgusted gesture I knew so well. It was late in the day to be making good my omissions, but not even Karel's ghost could stop me now. I reached up and put my mouth to the scarred side of his face. He began to flinch away, then was still and endured it like a punishment.

"You're wrong about that, Johannes. I can't tell you how wrong."

He shook his head. "Never mind, Tyl. It doesn't matter."

"It matters to me that I've let you believe it. It matters that I let you say, 'I want you so terribly to love me,' and I said nothing at all. You have a right to know these things. You have a claim on me."

"There are too many claims on you, Tyl. I would rather have none than see you made unhappy by them like this. I wanted things to be easier for you, not harder."

I had to close my eyes. I could no longer endure his kindness. Every word undermined me.

He said, "I want to help you, Tyl."

"You can. You can let me go on cheating. You can still be the camp commander and order me to come here. Because you see, it's the only way. I don't want to be free to come or stay away. Because if I am, they will never let me come."

"Who, Tyl?"

"Karel. And Piers and the fliers. The Blitzstein boy. People you never saw. A man who beat his brains out in the quarry. Tovah. Someone called Merz who was hanged on my first morning here—"

"Stop, Tyl!" With his good arm he drew me tightly to him. "Stop. You have too many dead." In the dark of closed eyes, my face against the black cloth of his uniform, there was a moment for quiet, for scarcely drawing breath. But there was to be no rest. He said, "This I cannot work out for you. You must do it for yourself. If I do what you ask it will only postpone it, not solve it. How much longer will we have here, do you think? A day or two? A week? And then? I'm more demanding than I was when I came here. I don't want a prisoner. I want you, free of your entourage of corpses, free to be a lover, a friend. I want you for the rest of my life, Tyl." He dropped his arm and stepped back to look down at my face. "I've refused you the only thing you've ever asked of me. Gabriel never taught me that love was such a hard discipline."

I said, "Don't do this to us, Johannes. I can't come back."

"Perhaps you can't. It's a chance I have to take. I can't share you with a dozen corpses any longer."

"I've shared you with one, and that's worse."

A smile did not get past the scarred corner of his mouth. "No, Tyl. Not for a long time now. Come back to me if you can, but come alone. You'll find me alone too."

"I won't be back."

"Don't make rash promises. Let's not drag this on any longer. It hurts too much. Good-by, Tyl. I shall love you all my life."

I said, "Good-by, sir," and returned to my side.

11

The Reds were prepared to celebrate my return with horded food and two cigarettes from Jacques. I told them to fuck off and lay down on my bunk with my back to them. They tolerated this with surprising meekness. I realized they thought I was still miserable about Karel.

The munitions factory had been bombed—accurately, at last—by the Americans. There was nothing for us to do but wait.

We could hear the Russian guns. The end of the war seemed so near that any delay, any silencing, even momentary, of those guns, was intolerable. For the first time since winter, people tried to escape. They were brought back but not punished.

The Reds were as intolerably restless as anyone, but Karel's old disciplines had got us through other springs and held. It surprised me that they matter-of-factly accepted me as Karel's successor. I was not at all eager for the responsibility and could not imagine how, behind my back as it were, it had come about. Franticek, it seemed to me, would have been the logical person. I said as much to Abri one night. He was the only person I could talk to without quarreling at that time.

He said "Karel didn't leave a will, but I think it's assumed that if he had done so he would have named you."

"Not if he had any sense."

"That's foolish."

He was doing a cat's cradle with a piece of string he had found. We were that bored that spring.

I lifted the web off his fingers, changing the pattern.

"You know about me, don't you, Abri?"

He took the string back. "I think so. It doesn't matter, you know. The possibility will never occur to Paul and Franticek."

"You mean things only matter if they're known about?"

"I mean you wouldn't be in a position to take over Karel's Mafia if it were known, simply because Paul and Franticek would never talk to you again."

"What about you, Abri?"

"Does it matter?"

"No."

"I don't find it difficult to understand. He's a very attractive person."

I was so startled I twisted the cat's cradle into a knot. Abri took it, unraveled it, and began a new one. "I don't mean sex," he said. "After Dachau all I want from sex is a long vacation, preferably for the rest of my life. General von Svestrom is attractive because he acknowledges his limitations and is at ease within them. That's a very rare, very attractive quality. Most people go batting against them all their lives, like moths who confuse windows with the open air. It's an ungraceful performance, and so silly, since only saints and geniuses ever manage to break through the glass."

"You're being very forbearing."

Once Abri had made me free of his mind and his secret. But I had chosen a different allegiance, and it would not happen a second time. He withdrew from my guilt with a mocking quotation. "Doesn't Nietzsche say somewhere that what is done in love is beyond good and evil?"

"I think Nietzsche is a shithead."

Abri smiled. "I think so too."

The rabbi now found himself in the awkward position of having to establish diplomatic relations with me. Considering that the last time we had talked he had wanted to put Karel out in the snow to die, he went about it with a wonderful lack of tact.

He said, "I was so sorry about Karel, Tyl. I know what it's like to lose a friend."

"Like Blitzstein," I wanted to say, remembering, as I always did, the helpless waif handed over to Colonel Shit's guards. I did not say it. The rabbi had never said I love you to Colonel Shit's successor. There was nothing I could now despise him for.

Another day and another, and the nights which were worse. The Russian guns seemed to move no nearer. Even knowing how mountains confuse sound and cheat distance it was intolerable not to know whether there was any progress at all. When Franticek suggested I go back to the camp commander's house and ask for permission to listen to the radio, I cut my fist to the bone against his teeth. We had a no-holds-barred fight all over the barracks, which left us bloody, bruised, and much less irritable than before.

It rained every day. After my fight with Franticek I went outside, not caring if I got soaked to the skin. I couldn't endure the barracks. I had got spoiled by the use of the camp commander's house.

I kept my back to that house. I went down to the edge of the camp where the gallows had once stood. The Danube Valley lay in a silver mist of rain. The mountains dripped. Christ, I was sick of mountains.

Still, it was better to be outside. The air smelled clean; of wet grass crushed underfoot and earth soft with rain. Water dripped into my face, running from my hair. I could cry now, I thought, and nobody be the wiser. But I couldn't. Since those long-ago nights after my father's letter arrived at St. Pölten I had lost the knack.

The rain stopped the way it had started, all in a breath. The clouds shredded and there was the sun and the blue sky. A ridiculous performance. Fucking show-off Austrian weather. Fucking Russian army, why didn't they get a move on? Now that the rain had stopped I could hear their guns again. They seemed no nearer. Hurry up, damn you!

"Hello, Tyl. Wet enough for you?"

"Hello, Jasper." Go away, you bore me. Everybody bores me. Most of the guards had grown polite and amiable over the last weeks. But Jasper had always been nice, so I didn't say it.

"Scenery," he said, looking with contempt over the checkerboard fields to the silver-threaded Danube. "Like a tourist poster, isn't it? See scenic Austria. Where I come from it's nothing but fields of potatoes and turnips. It's brown and flat and I can't wait to get back to it."

"East Prussia's like that. Just different shades of brown. Woods and moraines and lakes. Whole armies have got lost in it."

"Will you go back there, Tyl?"

"No."

He nodded sympathetically. He probably thought it was because of the Russians. Few people, inmates or guards, I had discovered, shared Karel's happy anticipation of the Red Dawn.

I saw Martin Lenz walking toward us across the meadow. Christ, what was this, a meeting of the camp poofs?

"What will you do when you get out, Tyl?" He smiled at Lenz. They didn't greet each other.

"I don't know. I can't think past the gate. If I drop dead one step past I won't mind a bit. I'll have walked out of here."

"I can understand that," said Jasper.

"Like hell."

"You think we are any less sick of this place than you are?"

"Please, you make me cry."

Lenz laughed. I said, "What are you going to do, Martin?"

"I'm going home with Jasper."

A kick in the belly, a childhood fall out of a tree on one's back, unable to draw breath even to scream. I thought I would vomit. It passed. My breath came back. "If the Russians don't shoot you," I said to Jasper.

"Well, of course. Everything depends on that." As if I'd said, "If it doesn't rain."

"Martin, you can't!"

Lenz smiled. I could tell that this had been settled between them for so long, considered, argued, and filed away, that nothing from the outside could affect it.

"I didn't think *you'd* be shocked, Tyl."

"Christ, not that way. I don't give a shit if you like to screw Jasper or his dog. But spending one more minute than you have to with a camp guard, that shocks me."

Unperturbed, Jasper said, "I didn't volunteer for this job."

"You could have refused."

"And ended up at the Russian front, or Inside? That's a lot to ask of an average person. I've always done my best for you."

"Because Karel blackmailed you."

"You think so?"

"I know so."

"Why don't you use your head sometimes, Tyl? What do you think Karel had to blackmail me with after General von Svestrom got here?"

"Why did you let him think he was blackmailing you, then?"

"He wouldn't have trusted me unless he had some kind of hold over me."

"I don't get it."

"I'll try to explain. I didn't like Karel—no offense, Tyl—but I respected him. You see—here, in Dachau, wherever he was— he was one of the few who had a choice. He chose Inside. Not many people can do that. I've known a few others, a priest or two, some Communists, not many. So if Karel felt more sure of me, if he and his friends could have a few hours out of the day during which they didn't have to worry, that was all right with me."

"Honest to God, Jasper, when I listen to you, I expect heavenly choirs to start singing behind the clouds. Why didn't you likc Karcl?"

"Because he was a killer, for one thing."

"And you're not."

"Yes, I am too. But I'm reluctant about it."

"People are just as dead."

158

"It's like talking to the wall, talking to you, Tyl. Look, Karel wanted Weizeck dead because it was the only way to get you out of the quarry. I wanted him dead because of Martin, and the fliers wanted him dead because he was killing them off one by one. There were a lot of people mixed up in it, not just me. Sure I was the only one who could get the cyanide in his coffee, but I wasn't the only person responsible for killing him."

"I don't care who killed him. I just couldn't see you calling Karel a killer, as if you were St. Francis of Assisi or something."

"All right. Fair enough. Another thing I didn't like about Karel was what he did to you."

"He kept me alive, is that what you mean?"

"No, of course not. But for Karel everything was black and white, and he forced you to see things the same way. Karel never allowed for a mistake and he never allowed for a difference of opinion. You can get by like that in camp, better probably than you can with a sense of proportion. But you're going to have to live outside, Tyl, and for that it was a bad education. Life just isn't like that."

"Ye olde homespun philosopher."

There was no getting through his hide. He only smiled. "I'm a farmer, Tyl. There's two things besides hard work that make a good farmer: he doesn't cut off his nose to spite his face, and he doesn't waste things. Martin and I started as badly as could be. What we've made of it, saved from it, we'll keep. And we won't waste as much as five minutes of it because of some damned-fool theory that he's on one side and I'm on the other and the person I love is my enemy. Do you see?"

They stood, Jasper's hand on Martin's shoulder, their whole lives planned, never to love each other more than now, never less. I could see them, fifty years from now, grubbing away on Jasper's potato farm, perfectly content. They'd never feel the way I did now, but they'd never have what Svestrom and I had had. They wouldn't know what to do with it. I realized I did not envy them one bit.

"And they lived happily ever after," I said derisively.

"If the Russians don't shoot me," said Jasper and walked away.

The sunset was a garish picture postcard. Purple-streaked orange, the mountains flamed, topped off by a froth of pink cloud. Svestrom used to laugh so at the vulgarities of nature. We northerners are snobs, being the owners of marine sunsets in the best of taste.

"Do you really mind, Tyl?"

Martin made me jump. I thought he'd gone after Jasper. "Why should I? You aren't one of us. I've hardly ever talked to you before today."

"No. I appreciated that. Founding a poof society didn't appeal to me either."

I hoped the boy wouldn't start to grow on me at this late date. Then I remembered about Jasper. I said, "Have you always been —you know—poofed?"

"I don't know. I mean, I was only fifteen when I came to Dachau, and I never had any experience before that."

"What happens if you all of a sudden become a reformed character Outside?"

It didn't bother him at all. "It's a possibility," he agreed. "We both realize that. But it isn't something you can plan for, Tyl. Probably all kinds of surprising things'll happen Outside."

"What were you before?"

"Rich man's son in Berlin, like you. It wasn't much of a preparation for this sort of thing."

I did not protest that I was not a rich man's son from Berlin but a piece of Pankow, bones made of birchwood, hair of ship-chandler's rope, eyes of the gray Baltic sea. They don't understand about land and what is really taken away. They don't even know the difference between being uprooted and rootless.

I said, "It isn't much of a preparation for potato grubbing, either."

"It doesn't appeal to you at all, does it? You've no idea how wonderful it sounds to me."

"With Jasper?" A beggar sneering at the rich. I—dispossessed of Pankow, without friend, without lover.

"You know," said Martin, ignoring the sneer, "you and I are a fine example of the wandering Jew, German style. So assimilated that when they came after us with knives we didn't even know they meant us. We heard 'Jew' and thought of someone with a beard and a kaftan in a ghetto. Not of the *Herr Kommerzienrat* Lenz, heaven forbid. I suppose you're the most extreme example of it, but there are a lot of us. I envy people like Abri. At least they know what they're Inside for."

"Abri hates it."

"No, I don't believe that. He can't cope with the loss of it, that's all. Ten or twenty years from now he'll go back to it and it will all be there, waiting for him. He'll be home."

"If you don't have roots, nothing holds you down," I said.

"You have to have roots. People aren't birds to go flying off, free as air, because nothing holds them down. The trouble with us is, we were never Jews in any sense that anchored us, and we'll never be Germans again. So you see, Tyl, for us it has to be a person."

"A camp guard!"

"Jasper. I can't do that 'my side—your side' any more. I used to be good at it. When Jasper said we started badly he wasn't exaggerating. Dachau was a lot worse than Heiligendorf, even Heiligendorf before General von Svestrom came. I hated Jasper. I hated all the guards. Did Karel tell you about Dachau, Tyl?"

"Yes."

"Then you know. Karel always managed somehow. It's true that it's easier to get along in camp if you're single-minded. He used to just kind of grit his teeth an say, 'Survive, damn you.' I could never do that. I spent all my time planning to kill Jasper. I didn't mind if they hanged me for it afterwards or beat me to death or anything. Only I couldn't work out how to get the time to do it. Because I wanted it to be slow and painful, and there just wasn't any way to get privacy long enough to do it.

"Then one day I saw Jasper down by some trees at the edge of the camp. It was a terribly cold day, and there wasn't another person outside. I thought I could grab his gun and shoot him. I'd realized by then I'd never get the chance to torture him to death.

"He was just sitting on his heels, holding out his hand toward something. When I got close enough I saw he was throwing crumbs to a bird, a woodcock or a pheasant—"

His vagueness on this fitted his description of himself as a rich man's son in Berlin. I thought pigeons were probably the only birds he had ever seen up close. But Jasper was a country person, who knew how to handle animals with confidence and tact. It occurred to me that he had brought his knowledge to the handling of prisoners, who are more debased than animals at liberty and therefore more dangerous. Quite the boy, our Jasper, I thought, feeling the need to sneer, to keep admiration at bay.

"Jasper's gun was beside him," Martin said. "I could have reached it easily.

"Each time he threw the crumbs a little nearer, and the bird came a bit closer. In the end it sat right by his feet and ate from his hand. After it had finished and had run off, Jasper got up and saw me. He said, 'Have you been here long, Martin? You've been very quiet.' I realized I'd been holding my breath. Jasper picked up his gun and told me it was his afternoon off, but he hadn't felt like going into town, and we just stood there, sort of embarrassed, I think, and starting to smile a bit, and it came to me that I'd never seen him before. I couldn't have told you what color his eyes were or whether he was tall or short or anything. He'd just been a uniform, boots, a gun, and a killer dog. For weeks afterwards I tried to get back to that: the abstraction I could hate. But it never worked again. He was a person. From that to the way I feel about him now doesn't seem half as big a step as the one I took that afternoon when I suddenly saw a face and realized his eyes were brown. Can you understand that at all, Tyl?"

I put my hands on the barbed wire. "No."

"I used to wonder. You saw so much of General von Sve-strom. Not just nights but all day, all the time he helped you look after Karel and during the quarantine afterwards. Were you really always able to keep on hating him?"

My hands closed on the barbed wire until I could feel the tearing flesh and the warm, sticky blood.

"Yes," I said. "Always."

Johannes. Johannes!

In my bunk I run my torn hands along the splintered wood, craving the pain.

Are you awake? Smoking your messy cigarettes, pacing the room—nine steps lengthwise, six across, eleven on the diagonal. The first few nights I thought you wouldn't go through with it. I thought you would have to send for me. But you won't. I know that now.

Johannes, I said, "Yes, always," and not a single cock crowed for me anywhere.

There is something I would like to tell you. Something that happened this afternoon when I saw those two so Darby and Joan, so content. For the first time since you sent me away I was glad. Glad for what we had. Even though we'll never have it again.

The nights get worse. I didn't expect that somehow. I thought if I could get through the first few they'd get easier. But it doesn't matter. Not past the other thing, the being glad. I wouldn't change anything, Johannes. Not a single hour of ours.

Are you awake, my dearest? I wish I could tell you these things. I wish thoughts could reach out and touch.

Johannes, I love you.

Another morning. The last.

A sunrise as gaudy as the sunset the night before. The last.

A red sunrise brings rain and the sound of guns—from the wrong direction.

At 10:17 A.M. our liberators arrive. Karel, Karel, what would you have said had you lived to see that they were not the Red Army but Americans, a spearhead of Patton's army on its way to rescue, of all things, the Imperial horses of Vienna's Spanish Riding School?

Well, they rescued us on the way, and it was fine watching our erstwhile guards being marched off at the end of a bayonet. The worst ones had disappeared days before, but none of them were universal favorites, and there was quite a bit of cheering.

A young American lieutenant with a bandaged hand took some of his men into Heiligendorf and went from house to house, commandeering food and clothes. He came back with a truckload full of clothes which he turned over to us. It wasn't a very efficient way of dealing with the situation and resulted in a mad scramble and some very peculiar choices. Paul, who is at least six feet tall, captured a midget's Sunday suit, while Dieter, who is only about my height, managed to grab an overcoat that touched his toes. I did not take part in the battle for the clothes. I knew what I would take.

Everyone had cheered when the guards were marched away, but no one said anything when the young American lieutenant went toward the camp commander's house, a carbine ready in the crook of his arm and a look on his face as if he were about to arrest Heinrich Himmler in person.

When they came out together the carbine was slung over the lieutenant's shoulder, Svestrom was speaking to him in English, and both were laughing. The lieutenant called over his driver, and both went over the story again. The other Americans too came to listen, and presently they were all looking at the Mercedes and laughing. I knew Svestrom was telling them about his bargain for the Christmas pig and asking them to let the farmer have his car.

Little Rosenblum corrupted camp discipline by calling out, "Good-by, Sir General. Good luck," after which quite a lot of the prisoners crowded around to say good-by and shake hands. God knows what the Americans made of it. One of them brought

Svestrom's things and put them in the back of the jeep. Svestrom turned back once more and looked over the camp.

I was alone, down by the river where we had buried Karel. He saw me and, taking in the implication of my having chosen to be at Karel's grave at that time, he smiled. He was a good loser, having, God knows, had enough practice. He turned back to the Americans and got into the jeep. I watched it drive out the camp gates. Unfair, unfair, that on this, the happiest day of my life, my face should suddenly be wet and cold with tears.

Later I went to the camp commander's house. It was empty of his few possessions: the uniforms, the brandy, and the books. But in the closet I found, as I had known I would, the gray flannels and blue wool shirt and Gabriel's Afrika Korps tunic. Though I called him for a long time, Marx did not come and I never saw him again.

An American soldier came instead and asked me if I was looking for something. He knew as much German as I knew English, and our conversation was limited. He asked me how it had been and I shrugged. Even if I had spoken English like a native, what was there to say? The American sniffed and said, "Carbolic," and I said "Typhus," two words we had in common. He retreated but paused politely in the doorway. "Cheer up," he said. "Your troubles are over. You are free—*frei*—you understand?" I said yes, I understood.

It turned out we were not so free as all that. The young lieutenant, who spoke German fairly well, called us together and told us we would have to remain at the camp for a few days longer. We would be fed and looked after, of course, and would presently be taken in charge by appropriate agencies for the purposes of repatriation et cetera. He was sure we appreciated the fact that we could not suddenly be let loose on the countryside without papers and identification. Besides, the Russians were fighting somewhere in the area near Vienna and we would be safest where we were. He was sure we understood.

I called a conference by Karel's grave. We met there, outside the circle of light cast by the bonfire, sick from eating too much food. I said, "We're going to fuck off tonight. I'm not staying here another night, Yanks or no Yanks."

"Where to?" asked Paul.

"Vienna. I want to see what the Red Dawn is like."

"What about not having identification like the American said?" asked Dieter.

Franticek touched his too-short sleeve and said, "We have identification."

"We'll get papers, Dieter," I said. "Don't worry. I'll look after you."

"When do we leave?" asked Franticek.

"Now. Steal us some food, get Rosa, and we're off. No point in waiting around."

"Has anyone seen Marx?" asked Abri.

"No, I looked for him before."

"Probably gone off in Svestrom's pocket," said Abri. "A Nazi cat."

"Let's go."

We were not the only prisoners to escape that night. Others had taken to the woods before us. At dawn we found five of the camp guards hanged by their ankles from the trees, their throats cut. Four of them were the kind of guards who had had every reason to take their chance in the woods. The fifth was Jasper.

12

A few miles from Vienna we ran into the Russian army. When we told them where we were from, they were very good to us, shared their food, let us ride on their tanks, and gave us carbines to shoot Austrian civilians with. Franticek and Paul turned out to be surprisingly accurate shots. Dieter tried to imitate them but hadn't the first idea how to go about it. He almost cried with vexation. I, remembering that I was only by accident on the side of the angels, held my fire.

There was not much left of the Elie house. The shelling of Vienna had wrecked everything but a piece of their library, the kitchen, and the cellar. The present occupants had moved some furniture into the cellar and lived, by Vienna standards, not uncomfortably.

They were an elderly couple: he a party functionary of some importance, she a corseted bitch who carried off, unsuccessfully but with great energy, the pretense that she had been born and bred here.

I told them they had ten minutes to get out. He merely gaped, but she was quite ready to do battle. "And who might you be?" she drawled through her nose, half great-lady-fallen-on-hard-times, half purest Lerchenfeld.

I couldn't see any point in explanations. We still had the carbines the Russians had given us, and I for one was quite ready to use mine.

She got the message all right. She wasn't a stupid woman. She told her husband, who had just caught on and was starting to bluster, to shut up, and then returned to us, very polite suddenly, addressing us as "young sirs." She wanted time to pack up their stuff. "Otherwise," she said, "what will become of us? We are old and we have nowhere to go."

"The Elies were old too. But of course they had somewhere to go. Did you worry about them?"

"The Elies?"

"The people whose house you are living in."

"But, young sir, they were Jews."

If she hadn't said that I guess I would have let them take their stuff. But now I just said, "Fuck off. In the clothes you are wearing. This minute."

"Such language!" She really was invincible. She almost made me laugh.

"Beat it," I said, "or you'll go without the clothes you're wearing."

She knew I meant it. Packing her husband under one elbow she made off. At the corner of the street she turned and shouted, "Hooligans! Gangsters!" Franticek gave them a blast from his carbine. The husband jumped three feet in the air, but I think he was just surprised, not hit.

We looked through what was left of the house. We found that the former occupants had left behind a good deal more than clothes. The kitchen was stocked with tinned Polish ham, Russian caviar, and French truffles. There was wine. There was jewelry. She had two fur coats.

We traded everything. The Vienna black market was booming. Abri and I went through what was left of the library. Many of the books were singed at the edges and smelled of smoke, but they were legible. It was a gentlemanly, conservative library and pleased Abri more than it did me. I didn't really start to read until I met Migaud, who is responsible, along with Michael, for what education I have.

Our black-marketeering was instantly and spectacularly successful. All our training at Heiligendorf had been directed toward this, after all. We were superbly educated for crime. We stole like magpies, lied with the most truthful faces in the world, and had no scruples about anything we did. Vienna owed us a living.

We traded the former owner's portrait of Hitler, autographed copy of *Mein Kampf,* and German flag to the Americans for souvenirs. This turned out to be so lucrative that we scavenged through half of Vienna for relics of the *Anschluss.* Most people were delighted to be rid of the stuff without running the danger of being seen by a nosy neighbor putting *Mein Kampf* into the garbage or trying to burn the German flag. The Yanks paid us with food, cigarettes, and clothes, which fetched just about any price we cared to ask. I still have a Watteau drawing given me be a desperate *Herrenreiter* for a pack of Camels.

In a peculiarly underground way we lived high on the hog. We had all the food, drink, and cigarettes we wanted, but we lived in a house without walls or water. We wore the clothes we had acquired at Heiligendorf (it doesn't do for black marketeers to look too prosperous, and I, of course, had my private reasons for keeping mine), but we dealt in museum paintings and Fabergé diamonds. We slept in army sleeping bags with Vienna's most expensive tarts. Yes, I too.

I had two reasons, both of them silly. One was financial. At seventeen I was able to afford girls that ex-tycoons and profiteers were gnashing their false teeth over. It went to my head. And I was curious about myself. I wanted to discover who I would have been without Svestrom. Had my first sexual experience been the casual playing around at school, or had Svestrom been what I had at first forced him to be;—a queer camp commander who had ordered a prisoner to keep his bed warm— my past would not have presented me with a puzzle. Any purely sexual encounter tells the truth about the body. It is only love which confuses us.

I have to laugh at it now, but I even had a proper mistress for a while. She was not a tart, she was three years older than I,

169

she had tawny hair and golden eyes. It was like having a lioness in bed. Unfortunately she found nothing better to do with her time than to fall in love with me, and a lioness in love with one is an uncomfortable proposition.

Her name was Serena. What a misnomer! The scenes she made, indefatigably, tears and honey hair streaming. Of course I can see where I wasn't a very satisfactory lover for her, owned more completely than a slave, because owned in mind and heart as well as body by a man she did not even know existed.

There were men, too: one bad, one wonderful, most of them indifferent. The bad one was my first since Heiligendorf. I met him at an American party, where I discovered that I had no talent for strong drink. It's not much fun to wake up in the morning with the world's most spectacular hangover, in bed with someone one doesn't remember and doesn't like the looks of.

Unfortunately he didn't share my lack of memory. In fact he seemed to have total recall, so that sick and suicidal I rolled back into Serena's sleeping bag for a few more weeks, until Michael got me unstuck from that particular gluepot.

Michael, my *semblable,* my not quite twin. Abri found him for me, saying, "You have a doppelganger who eats lunch at the Golden Fleece—you know, the restaurant around the corner from Bidermann Theater. He's an actor."

"I didn't know doppelgangers ever ate. I thought they just stood on your doorstep and wrung their hands."

"Go see," said Abri. "Maybe he's a long-lost relation."

I left Abri to autograph a stack of copies of *Mein Kampf* (the signature increased their black market value considerably) and went around to the Bidermann Theater to check. There was no Pankow or Elie listed among the cast. The last thing I wanted to do was to run into a long-lost relation.

I did not take any further steps about my doppelganger just then. I was busy charming the pants off General Hess, a sport about as harmless as going swimming with a shark. It didn't allow for divided interests.

General Hess had recently been put in charge of the Vienna

Military Police. He had been preceded by a reputation for a violent temper, wild eccentricity, and peculiar passions. The Vienna underworld foresaw a halcyon future of blackmail and chicanery. Unfortunately for them, General Hess exercised his eccentricities and passions so blatantly that blackmail became redundant. The chicanery came only from his side.

How he had ever become a general in the American army was a mystery. Probably nobody had ever got up enough nerve to suggest retirement to him. And admittedly he did his work with breath-taking efficiency.

To render him harmless was impossible. I could only hope to make him amiably disposed toward me and to direct his chicanery toward my enemies. It was an enterprise which at first absorbed all my attention. Not until I felt safe did I remember to inspect my doppelganger.

I took Serena around to the Golden Fleece to have lunch. "It smells like a damp goat," she said, the only remark I can remember her making which was both true and funny.

He was there. Not a doppelganger, really; no one ever mistook one of us for the other. He was much better looking, for one thing: older, less ordinary, more dramatic. This should have made him resemble Gabriel rather than me, but he was me all right.

It startled me to see him, but at least I had expected it. He hadn't. Someone at his table pointed me out to him: "Don't look now but there's someone over there—" Of course he looked. He looked, in fact, extremely surprised. He dithered for a moment, made up his mind, and came over to our table.

He wore a ski paratroop jacket, patched at the elbows, and a pair of marvelous prewar ski pants. He said, "My name is Michael Dehn. Could we be relatives?"

"Mine is Pankow and I don't have any relatives."

"What an enviable state."

"This is Countess Serena von Hajos-Janoshalma."

"*Epatant,*" said Michael.

We finished our lunch together, spent the afternoon walking

and talking, lost Serena somewhere along the way without noticing, went to Michael's play—*Fiorenza,* that night—walked Michael home in the streaming rain, walked me home to the opposite end of town, walked Michael home, put our cards on the table, and went to bed.

Serena tracked us down by noon the next day, finding us still in bed, drinking coffee. Eyes and hair streaming, she made her farewells and overturned the coffeepot into the bed. I was extremely embarrassed (why, for heaven's sake?), but Michael watched her histrionics with professional interest. After she left, he said, "Do you think she'll drown herself in the Danube? There's a definite Ophelia air about her. All that hair! It would be most becoming."

(She didn't. I ran into her recently. She had an American colonel in tow, a Russian sable on her back, and a French poodle on a leash. She looked quite recovered. *He* looked like a secret queer to me, but that may be an unworthy thought.)

Michael said, "You lead a confused life, Tyl."

"I know. It confused me too. But I think I'm unconfused now."

"Good. I love you, I think."

Dismayed, I said, "No. Oh no, don't. I'm not that unconfused."

"I have no choice. You are my twin and my mirror."

This begins to sound like the fatuous catalogue of a successful lover. How I wish it were. But in fact no one has ever loved me —Tyl. Johannes loved Gabriel, Michael loves Michael. Serena? God knows what she even meant by the word. Her own emotions. Instant *grandes passions*. To Serena a lover is someone she can scratch her initials on. When she didn't succeed with me, I think she became obsessed with her lack of success. (Migaud says, "To be wholly owned by one thing is to be free of all others. The appearance of freedom, however spurious, is very attractive to people. They want the secret, and by falling in love with the person who has it, they think they can obtain it.")

A Schoenberg quartet played in a roofless lecture room at the university, *Ubu Roi* read in a restaurant between lunch and dinner, a cubist show (very bad, this) in a railway waiting room, a Camus performance in a cellar, a Brecht rehearsal, a meal snatched from a sausage stall, an amateur and amateurish performance of *Der Jasager* which left me close to tears: Michael's Vienna.

For me, who had grown up during the twelve drab years when Picasso was a *Kulturbolschewist,* Freud a Jewish pornographer, and Brecht a Communist as well as a Jew, it was more intoxicating than drugs or drink.

One afternoon I outlined a set design for *The Good Woman of Szechuan* on the tablecloth with a finger dipped in red wine (Oh, seacoasts of Bohemia!), and Bidermann gave me my first job and first success.

In my notebook, between the sketches of *Good Woman,* I wrote down incidents of my life with Michael. I tend to lose my notebooks and am careless about even the most intimate letters and diaries, but these trivia for some reason I have left.

Tragedy at the movies. *The Bridge of San Luis Rey.* Michael says, "I saw an earlier version of this. One of the first talkies, I think it was. I fell madly in love with Lily Damita. I decided to become an actor so that I could meet her some day. Of course I never have."

Thoughtlessly, forgetting Michael's obsession that twenty-five is the beginning of old age and thirty senility, I ask, "Who on earth was Lily Damita?"

Michael, turning into the aged and stricken Charlus of *Le temps retrouvé* before my eyes, says tragically, "This morning I was a beautiful young man. Tonight I am an aged pederast. I will *never* go to the movies with you again."

As for scenes, Serena could learn from Michael any day. Of a distinguished critic: "How dare that scrofulous son of a syphilitic whore give five paragraphs to your sets and only two to my acting!"

At the stage door a group of giggling girls asks for my autograph. I sign Michael's name obligingly, until he himself appears, wearing his beautiful Boeckl ski pants, his face dramatic with smudges of carelessly cleaned make-up. The gigglers, furious, hurl themselves upon him with their pens.

Michael gets a lot of love letters from adoring females. We divide these between us and I help him answer them.

Michael says making love between rehearsal and performance is good for his acting. Making love between black market deals is good for me, but bad for the deals.

Abri hands me Verlaine's contemptuous line: *Rires et jeux, ou besoins érotiques.*

It doesn't bother me at all. I've been miserable long enough. I'm ready for laughs and games, and as for the *besoins,* Michael suits them perfectly. In fact, in the limited sense of "fun," I enjoy myself more with Michael than I ever did with Svestrom. There is no passion, no terror; not enough of me is involved for it to matter whether it's a success. For that reason, probably, it invariably is.

I have stopped biting my nails.

Homosexuality as camp politics, says Franticek, is commendable. But for fun it is vice, perversion, and reactionary decadence, properly and sternly condemned by the Party.

It all surprised me very much.

"It shouldn't," says Michael. "It's the normal way of looking at it."

"How do you mean, normal?"

"Well, average. I realize your education has some astonishing gaps in it, but that is something your Johannes really might have warned you about."

The shock winded me. "How do you know about Johannes?"

"You talk in your sleep."

"The one thing I am absolutely sure of is that Johannes never had the faintest idea what went on in an average person's mind."

Once, in answer to some remembered headmaster idiocy, he said, "Of course it can ruin your life. So can heterosexual passion, a passion for power, drink, money, drugs—"

"Is it the passion that's wrong, then?" I remember asking.

He said, "No. The lack of proportion, I think. Using a prism to see only one color."

"Tell me about Johannes, Tyl. Who was he?"

A man in pain. A man in love. A drunk, often. A man who had lost the gift of sleep, but watched the larks at dawn. "A man I used to be in love with," I say. "There's nothing to tell."

Henry IV at the Bidermann. Michael a beautiful Prince Hal. The translation and sets could stand a lot of improvement, though. I can't do anything about the translation, but I'll ask Bidermann to let me do new sets. I've got a hundred ideas, all of them wonderful.

Franticek, Abri, Verlaine, and the Communist Party can jump into the Danube. I know something none of them know: it is possible to have a successful love affair without being in love.

Bedtime, Hal. All's well.

That is the end of the journal I kept of my life with Michael. It's not very long, but it is complete. I never designed sets for *Henry IV*. Heiligendorf, that filthy dungheap, did not let me go. After I blew a deal with General Hess, the Reds lost patience with me and handed me the ultimatum, "Him or us." I said "You" without a moment's hesitation.

I'm a coward about good-bys. I left Michael with the whore's trick of a note on the pillow.

Lord, I miss him!

13

Migaud scolds me. "Why do you waste your time here? *Il faut protéger le talent.*"

"What's the good of that? The only thing worth protecting is genius. And genius doesn't need it."

"You combine the three cardinal faults. You are Prussian, Protestant, and Puritan."

I can't resist the alliteration, "And *putain.*"

"How you flatter yourself."

They say he used to be humbly Mirko Halasz, a middle European who on his own initiative made good God's oversight in not letting him be born a Frenchman. Certainly his French is terrible. I think he gets it all out of one of those phrase books for tourists.

I came here for the first time at the end of last November. It seems impossible that it should be only a few months ago. I feel as if I had known Migaud all my life.

I'd heard of him, of course, from the moment I arrived in Vienna. Behind every major operation—not the pimps tipped into the Danube at night or the prostitutes cheated out of a day's pay—behind the big, elegant crimes that empty bank vaults and museums, one arrived always at Migaud.

In November I heard through the underground grapevine that Migaud felt his life was not complete without the collaboration of General Hess. Unfortunately General Hess was fiercely and possessively guarded by his adjutant. To see General Hess alone one had to be a lot younger and better-looking than Migaud.

I had grown very tired of the adjutant myself. Because he was not very intelligent, he had so far been content to be my tame M.P. But it had at long last dawned on him that there was little point in a mere percentage when you could take over the whole business. And the galling fact was that there was nothing to prevent him from doing so. He could simply walk in, arrest us for black-marketeering, and confiscate all our loot. I decided to suggest tactfully to Migaud that the road to General Hess was over the dead body of the adjutant.

Migaud's bar was then located, as a sop to the curfew, behind an ordinary apartment door. But I am sure there wasn't a faggot in Vienna ignorant of its location.

I had thought association with Michael's friends had disabused me of the quaint idea acquired from Svestrom that queers are just like everybody else when they are not in bed. But Migaud's bar was a shock. It looked and sounded like the parrot house in the zoo. Michael's most flamboyant friends were drabs by comparison with Migaud's clientele.

When I introduced myself, Migaud was delighted for the wrong reason.

"*Enchanté,* Tyl Pankow. So that is who you are. And I thought you were merely a clever black marketeer."

"What do you mean, that is who I am?"

"So modest, and yet you caused quite a little stir recently. The young Rimbaud of the Bidermann Theater, and just as badly behaved, from all one hears."

"How do you hear all that nonsense?"

"How do I hear? I have kept track of you, of course. You see, I am interested in painting, and I went to see the sets. Only it never occurred to me that the Tyl Pankow who designed them was the black marketeer as well. The sets were beautiful. Alas, the play was not. Someone really ought to point out to the good Bidermann that being banned by the Nazis is not in itself a guarantee of quality. *Après tout,* they banned syphilis, didn't they? However, your sets were well worth two hours of Herr Brecht's drivel. You're one of the lucky ones, aren't you? The ones who don't have to sweat for it. The Mozarts, not the Beethovens. The ones who cheerfully write poems in jail, compose songs in the dentist's waiting room, and paint masterpieces on brown paper bags with their children's watercolor sets."

"You overestimate me on both counts. I don't have any children and I don't paint masterpieces. Except for the Bidermann sets and a few drawings, I've done nothing worth mentioning."

"So I suspected. The great danger to people with your kind of talent is that it lacks urgency. Easy come, easy go. You dawdle and waste time and cheat your talent because you know it will still be there when you're ready to go back to it. But the question is, will *you* be there? Modigliani, Van Gogh, Toulouse-Lautrec, Seurat all died in their thirties. The thirties are dangerous years for painters. If they last till they're forty they'll probably also last to eighty. It's the thirties they must watch out for. Show me your hand." He took it, palm up. Then he said, "You'd better get busy. You'll not see eighty, nor forty for that matter, with a life line like that. Stop wasting your time trading cigarettes and designing sets for an ass like Bidermann, who thinks a play is good if it is written by a Communist."

"He does Shakespeare too, you know."

"Well, after all. Shakespeare, *Faust, Nathan der Weise,* they are *de rigeur*. They do not require much imagination. I'm sure he'd much rather be doing a dramatized version of *Das Kapital*. He wastes your time."

"I'm not working for him. I only did the Brecht."

"Good. Then you can get busy on the things that matter. Pictures, Tyl Pankow. Paintings. Not cardboard chinoiseries for the actors to trip over."

Over the bar he had hung an ink drawing of a lady walking a dog. An unbroken black line, brilliant with mockery and laughter.

"You admire my Toulouse-Lautrec," said Migaud.

"Is that who painted it? He was a cripple, wasn't he?"

"Yes. Does it matter?"

"Probably not, if he could do this." It seemed to have been drawn in a single breath; the bell-shaped skirt afloat with the movement of the swift walk Lautrec himself had never known, the leash and dog an exclamation point of joy.

"Buy you a drink, sweetie?"

The standard uniform: tight ski pants, a brilliantly colored sweater, green eye shadow.

"Screw you."

"Yes, please."

Why do I despise them? Because I don't wear eye shadow and don't call anybody sweetie?

Migaud listened to bitcheries, gave advice to the lovelorn, settled quarrels, and served his washy beer. (He calls it *rince-cochon* in his hit-or-miss French.) Later, when I knew him better, I drew a caricature of him, dressed in a nanny bonnet with streamers, supervising his flamboyant and despairing nursery. He tacked it up next to the Lautrec: the best compliment I've ever had, from the one person whose judgment I respect.

Just before the bar closed he said to me, "Don't leave. I have something to show you." He shooed out the late-stayers, unlocked the door to his apartment, and turned on the lights. What he wanted to show me, of course, were his paintings: the red Matisse which filled an entire wall, two Modigliani nudes, a Cézanne teapot, a beautiful early Kandinsky, three Picassos, and a small Vermeer, worth a million dollars a square inch, unbuyable, unpayable. These were his favorites. Others were stacked on wide shelves built all around the room, the most magnificent plunder of the war.

"Copies, of course," said Migaud, "but rather good ones, I think. No private collector nowadays could afford the originals."

The lie was his insurance, since the paintings were hardly insurable in the normal way. Had he shown me diamonds or first editions I'd probably have gone along with it. For one thing I couldn't have been positive that he was lying. But about paintings I found myself saying, "Copies, my ass."

"*Tiens!* What makes you think they are originals?"

"I don't think. I know it."

"Well, tell me how you know it."

"A painting is like a human being. It starts with a conception. You can't see it on the canvas any more than you can see the egg which becomes the child. But if they ever manage to make a robot that's an exact replica of a person you'll still know it's not human. It's the same thing with a painting."

"*Bon,*" said Migaud. "You are young and you have no tact, but youth improves with the years and tactlessness must be forgiven the artist."

"Please don't call me an artist."

"Come, come, I have seen those sets you did for the good if boring Bidermann. You see, Tyl, I cannot draw at all, not even the little rabbit like an egg with a question mark for a tail that children make in kindergarden. But I can recognize a talent when I see it. I don't know how I do it exactly; the same way you recognized that my paintings were originals, I imagine. I am never wrong. Now, have some brandy and tell me how you managed to meet General Hess, how I can manage to meet General Hess, and what you want for the information. That is what you came here for, is it not?"

So I told him. When I left at four in the morning it was with a copy of *Une saison en enfer* under my arm and the advice which was to grow so hatefully familiar: "Work. *Il faut protéger le talent.*"

A few weeks later, bypassing the adjutant, I arranged a meeting between Migaud and General Hess. That they should become each others' greatest admirers was a foregone conclusion. Their enthusiastic friendship gave the adjutant much heartburn and me a great deal of pleasure (and profit). It also brought about the end of my life as a criminal, for the adjutant never forgave me. He waited until I had, with Migaud's help, pulled off the most profitable deal of my career and, before I could get rid of the profits, dropped on me and collected the lot. He had it planned, of course, that he would take us off to jail where we couldn't get back at him, but at that we balked and showed our credentials as Heiligendorf graduates. The adjutant thought it over and chose the next best thing to a life sentence: he gave us to Captain Aspinall. I wanted Migaud to tie the adjutant to a stake in the Danube and let him congeal by degrees, but Migaud, that loyal friend, said that I had been careless, that my heart was not in my work, that General Hess was unaccountably fond of the adjutant and he, Migaud, was unaccountably fond of General Hess, besides which suffering enriches the artist and daily contact with Captain Aspinall would be good for my painting.

It is very late—very early—the suicide hours (as if I ever would, knowing J. alive), and we are on the other side of the door, the bar empty and silent, Migaud's room filled with the red Matisse on the wall.

When General Hess is here he always sits with his back to the Matisse—I don't know anything about art, but I know what I like—causing Migaud to yelp with anguish.

"I suspect you are not truly *pédéraste*," says Migaud. "You work too hard at it."

"Possibly." It's not a question I ever expect to find a definitive answer to.

They say Migaud has no sex life at all. That he never bothers with lovers, women, boys, except to buy and sell. He's no beauty, but that's not the answer. Abri is so beautiful that after seeing him every day for nearly four years it still makes my heart stop to come unexpectedly upon him. And he's always alone. How do they live?

I'm half pissed on Migaud's brandy, which I don't like and have no head for, and only drink to be polite (and because it reminds me of J.), so I ask him.

He says, "Sex is for dirty children. *Les enfants sales*."

"Did you call *me* a puritan?"

"Sex is for puritans too. They are not grown up."

"What is for grownups then?"

"Crime and art."

Tomorrow is my eighteenth birthday. Migaud casts my horoscope. Pisces: two fish lashed together in the sky, attempting to swim in opposite directions.

Migaud says, "Avoid disreputable friends, depressing thoughts, and feelings of revulsion. Most great painters are born under your sign. Work!" He refuses to read my palm. "It depresses me."

"Because my life line is so short?"

"I beg of you, do not make me these *fadaises*. How long a life line do you think Modigliani had? Or Schubert, or Rimbaud? Look, do you see this deep line you have down the center of your left hand? That is your line of talent, accomplishment, success. In your left hand are the lines you were born with. The right hand shows what you do. What has become of that line? Waste always depresses me. *Il faut protéger le talent*."

"I'll send you my ear first thing in the morning."

"Madness is not a requisite of talent. Neither, for that matter, is perversion."

"Captain Aspinall worries about me too."

"Captain Aspinall worries about the things you do. They revolt me, but they do not worry me. I worry about the things you do not do."

As a matter of fact, Aspinall does too. It bothers him that I spend my days doing nothing, scrounging his cigarettes, playing with Rosa, watching the snow fall. It's only at night that I can't be at rest. Aspinall knows I get out, of course. He pretends he doesn't because it's illegal, he knows I can trick him fifty ways he's never thought of, and most of all he doesn't want to know what I do outside.

But I can't get through the nights alone. And I don't want another Michael. It involves too much and hurts the wrong people. Strangers are safe.

I remember Michael saying once, over a penitential breakfast of tea and dry toast, "Two things give me a hangover. Too much champagne and too much sex." I get hung over from not sleeping. It panics me and I get sick and frantic. Yet I know one can't work at forcing sleep. It comes only at moments of inattention. And these I can achieve only in a strange bed, against a stranger's arm.

When I leave, Migaud comes downstairs with me. He says, "Love is every kind of hell there is, and sex is a *bétise*. Go home and go to bed, Tyl. Alone. *Sois sage*."

"All right, Migaud."

"Good night."

In the street a shadow takes shape and moves toward us. "Tyl?"

"And to think you have not even invented a better mousetrap," says Migaud, exasperated.

"Michael!" A moment's panic, then only delight. "I'm so glad to see you."

Migaud slams the door.

"I seem to have been tactless," says Michael acidly.

"No. It's not what you think. How did you find me?"

"That at least was easy. You're the talk of the town."

"Don't be an ass."

"Well, our part of the town. Quite the celebrity. Tyl, the inscrutable. Tyl, the untouchable. Tyl, the available enigma."

"You're drunk, Michael."

"A little. I wouldn't have come, sober. Why, Tyl? Why do you do it?"

"I can't sleep."

We are on a bridge. Under us, darkness and the rushing of water. Michael leans over the railing and drops his cigarette into the dark. "You slept when you were with me."

I have nothing to say. It's true.

"Look, Tyl, I don't believe in having pride about these things. The only thing pride gets you is your bed to yourself most of the time. Tyl, why all the others? Why not me?"

"Because they're strangers."

"That's the answer? That's all?"

"It's all I understand. The rest is Heiligendorf."

"Heiligendorf. How will you ever leave it?"

"I went back once, you know."

"Did you? I didn't know."

"I never told anyone." I do not tell anyone now.

Heiligendorf is a DP camp now. There are at least five hundred people where two hundred were overcrowded. Some are old and ill. There are children. But they seemed to be warmly dressed and did not look starved.

The farmers' wives from the village go there for their Sunday walk. They never did that when we were there. They bring food and hand it past the barbed wire. Like a zoo. Except the animals are human.

It started to rain, the afternoon I was there. The DPs had run for cover. The sightseers had gone home with their prams and string bags. There were only two of us left: me, and the boy on the other side of the fence, his hands clenched on the barbed wire, blood running down into his sleeves.

I used to wonder, flattered and terrified, what about me had made Karel include me, a newcomer, into his group. Now I knew.

I said, "I ran away from here once. I can come back at dark and show you how."

"I know how."

His eyes were the same color as mine. I wished he were my brother. "Come to Vienna with me."

"I'd like that. But I can't. My father is here. He's sick."

"Your father. Do you care?"

"Yes. They'd let him die. I have to stay."

He reached across the barbed wire and we shook hands. When I got back to Vienna his blood had dried on my fingers.

Michael does not prod. We walk in silence till we come to my door.

"Is this where you live now? How imposing."

"It belongs to the Yanks." My description of Captain Aspinall makes him laugh.

"I'm glad you found me, Michael. I missed you."

"A cold comfort for a cold bed. All right, Tyl, I won't nag. You're not the only available boy in Vienna, after all. But don't disappear again. It annoys people."

"I promise. Good night, Michael."

"It's almost morning. Will you come to the play tomorrow? It's *Fiorenza*. You always liked that."

It was the first play I had seen him in. Too much past. "I can't tomorrow. What's the day after?"

"*Galileo*."

"I've never seen that."

"You'll love it," says my old Michael. "I'm brilliant in it."

Five-thirty is still a safe time for coming back. After that the early risers begin to stir, and one must preserve the fiction that Tyl spends the night in his own bed.

Cold. And sick from not sleeping.

An envelope is on my pillow. It contains a key. Not a bedroom key, needless to say.

Grown-up Americans all write the way they were taught in school.

Captain Aspinall's note explains that this is the key to his office. He has a letter for me which he did not like to leave on the bed for fear it might get lost. The most wonderful news. He couldn't be happier for me. And what do I mean by not being in my room at 11 P.M.?

There are two letters. The second is not for me. The first, the one Captain Aspinall was in such raptures about, is from Stockholm. I know exactly what it says. They thought I was at school all along, they couldn't be more furious with the Rittmeister for not looking after me properly, herewith money and a ticket for Stockholm. I've been expecting it for weeks. It doesn't interest me.

The second letter is not addressed to me and has its top page missing. I have time for the fleeting thought that the only letters that have ever mattered to me are addressed to other people and don't have a first page.

My curiosity about Aspinall's correspondence is not strong and he is usually safe leaving his letters around. But the name leaps from the page (as names beginning with J or S always do, and usually disappoint), so I take a look.

. . . in charge of the investigation of a General von Svestrom who was the commandant of the Heiligendorf concentration camp, so I was particularly interested in your mentioning that you're working with some of the prisoners from there.

The case of General von Svestrom seems to be boiling down to a mere formality. Every witness who was there agrees that he only arrived in September '44 (a punishment for suspected participation in the July 20th plot, it seems) and that he did everything in his power to make the camp as tolerable as possible under the circumstances. It all sounds straightforward and simple, and how I wish I'd majored in psychology, like you, instead of wasting my time on history. This Svestrom has me beat.

What do you do with someone who will not exonerate himself, refuses to discuss any part of the past (I didn't even get the July 20th business from him, and you know that you can't meet a Nazi officer anywhere who wasn't according to himself involved in The Plot)? It's kind of embarrassing because there was a lot of red tape, so he was held by us for quite a while before anybody got around to him, and now it turns out we can't even denazify him because he was never a member of the party. "No one ever asked me to join," he said when I asked him how he'd managed that. "I imagine everyone assumed I already was a member." And when I asked him whether he would have joined if pressed to do so, he said, "Oh, surely," and I found I didn't believe a word of it.

Of course this whole denazification program is ridiculous. I was never so conscious of it as I am with this General von Svestrom. He says, "Why work so hard? Just accuse me of whatever you like." When I tell him the law doesn't work that way, he says, "Of course it does. On what other basis am I your prisoner?" What am I supposed to say to that? "Because you're a German officer and lost the war"?

He owns five books and a cat and, according to himself, nothing else, though a little investigation disclosed a widowed mother in Hanover, a castle, and an estate of feudal dimensions. If you want to know why he was allowed to keep a cat, all I can tell you is that the lieutenant who arrested him at Heiligendorf forgot who represented the winning side. And frankly, I've never quite had the nerve to point out to him that keeping a cat is under the circumstances highly irregular. Its name, by the way, is Marx, and what, if anything, I am supposed to make of that God only knows. He also owns a crippled arm, constant pain (I suspect), insomnia, and a fair share of the demons that are after anybody who's been through the fighting end of this war.

On the other hand he started it. I look at him sometimes in his handsome black uniform (tank corps, not SS) and I tell myself, I fought bastards like you all the way from Normandy, my father fought you in the last war, and if I have a son he'll probably have to take you on again twenty-five years from now. Why can't you Prussians leave the world alone?

And then I get to arguing his side for him since he won't. Whatever we like to think, it isn't only the Prussians who started this war. And maybe I've killed as many people as he has. Certainly this last year from D Day on I've scored a good number, while he spent that year from all reports but his own doing everything he could to keep alive as many of those poor bastards at Heiligendorf as possible and succeeding none too badly. The trouble with being a historian is that you get too much perspective on good causes. I mean, sure Hitler was mad and these Germans are monsters, but if I were to study the history of World War II five hundred years from now, would this justify to me the ruined countries, the millions dead and millions more crippled and starved, and Hiroshima—especially Hiroshima? I haven't, to tell you the truth, been in the full possession of my virtue since August 6.

Maybe everybody in uniform is guilty, and why am I sitting in judgment on a German officer?

There is another side to this argument, I know. There must be. I'll leave it to you to write it to me, the sooner the better, for as you can see the morale here is very low. Half the time I can't remember who the guilty party is. All I want to do is to get him out of here as fast and painlessly as possible (which I can) and to ease the demons up some (which I can't).

An illegible signature and an extenuating circumstance.

3:30 A.M. Up all night drinking with The Enemy.

I laugh and laugh, holding the letter, my fingers and face splashed with tears. Oh, God, Johannes, it's funny funny funny and I'm having hysterics, I think, but it doesn't matter. I'm holding a letter someone wrote after getting drunk with you.

Aspinall has left his cigarettes on the desk. I smoke them, one after the other, making a sloppy mess of each one as they dissolve from my tears.

I read the letter over and over and laugh more than I weep now at what you have done to the poor American. I'm glad you've got him, though. He sounds decent, and he's the first one I've come across who seems to have lost some sleep over Hiroshima. The awfulness of it, Johannes. It was Auschwitz all over again. I can't see any difference at all except that no one celebrated the existence of Auschwitz, but I saw a newsreel of everyone dancing and shouting and getting drunk in Times Square.

The cigarettes are finished, a soggy, revolting mess. I'm finished too; no more hysterics, no more tears. Just farewells to my ghosts. This is always their hour, the dawn, and they never fail me. Blitzstein and Merz and Piers, the strangled fliers and Tovah and the man who was shot for stealing a piece of bread. And I am at last ready to say to them, "You are dead. Get off my back."

But there is Karel still. I don't say it to him because I loved him and made him a promise which I am going to break. He wouldn't listen anyway.

It's funny that it took an outsider, an American, to make me see it at last. Jasper tried to tell me. But he was a camp guard, so I didn't listen. You caught me young and ignorant, Karel, and I believed what you taught me. You drew a line: Them—Us.

The bad Nazis and the good prisoners.

All right for you and Franticek and the fliers. Even for the Menshevik in 4C. But what about the rest of us? The possession of Jewish parents did not make us good; only, in this particular instance, innocent. How many of us, given a choice between being prisoner or jailer, would have chosen Inside? Me? Like hell.

Svestrom would have, I think.

Svestrom is not an enemy. Jasper was not an enemy. I am not an enemy. Not any more. The enemies, Karel, are the people who draw the lines. You are an enemy.

I owe you, probably my life, certainly my sanity, which matters more. But I paid that back. I chanced my life for yours. I owe you for a great deal of deceit and dishonesty. Maybe this year without Svestrom has paid for it. I think so. I'll owe you for a broken promise now. Nothing pays for that.

Collect the debt in any way you like, Karel. I admit I'm afraid of you. You don't have the makings of an easygoing bill collector, alive or dead. You'll get your own back.

But this is *my* own. *Protéger le talent* and Svestrom. I'll pay whatever you want for it. It's worth it.

I couldn't leave the letter behind, so I took it to bed with me. I fell asleep laughing, thinking of Aspinall's face if I said, "I'm going to live happily ever after with General von Svestrom," slept around the clock, and awoke with a workable plan in my head.

Aspinall was furious with me. For months he has closed his eyes to my deals with Migaud, my absences, the strangers in the street. But at last I have committed the unforgivable crime. I have read a letter not addressed to me.

The shape in which I returned it did not improve the situation. It was slopped with tears and bits of wet cigarettes, and crumpled from being held in my hand while I slept.

I felt wonderful. I'd slept for twelve hours. The morning taste of mint and cigarettes in my mouth made me hungry for coffee and bacon and eggs and toast; the kind of American breakfast that usually made me sick at the sight of it. I even liked Captain Aspinall.

"And what about this?" He held up my father's letter from Stockholm. "Is my mail so interesting to you that you can't be bothered to read a letter from your parents? What's the matter with you, Tyl?"

"I'm sorry about your letter. Look, I can explain it. I know I shouldn't have read it. But I couldn't help myself. The thing I really feel terrible about is those Pankows. It never occurred to me that anything like this would happen."

"What are you talking about, Tyl? Make sense."

"You'll be furious with me."

"I am furious with you."

"I know." He isn't really. He's enjoying this. "You want to repatriate me, don't you?"

"The sooner the better." He smiles to show that he does not mean it. "But how can I? I can't force you to go to East Prussia, and I won't send you to your grandfather."

"You don't have to." The moment of truth. "You see, Captain Aspinall, I'm not Tyl von Pankow."

"You're not? Then who on earth are you?"

I pause one more artistic moment. Should I confide in him or not? Confidence wins over doubt. I decide to speak the truth. (Thank you, Michael. I learned more about acting from you than I realized.)

"My name is Svestrom. General Svestrom is my father."

"What?"

"Scout's honor." In case there is still a lingering doubt, I douse it with my most candid look and the final argument. "Look at me, Captain." Straw-colored hair falling into gray Pankow (or Elie) eyes. "Do I look like a Jew?"

That does it. The rest is just technicalities.

Why the masquerade? I was ashamed of my father. How would you like it if somebody in your family ran a concentration camp? But now I'm ashamed of having been ashamed. Parents are parents, after all, and families should be together.

What about those Pankows?

I really feel terrible about them. Honestly, it's awful. I never thought things would turn out like this. There was a Pankow at the camp, but he died. Also, while we are putting our cards on the table, I am not nineteen. (Aspinall has no reason to know Svestrom's age, but just in case he should find out I want my story to be at least remotely plausible.)

This confirms a suspicion he has long harbored, says Captain Aspinall. I don't look nineteen to him. Am I not ashamed to have been such a liar?

I am ashamed and promise not to do it again.

My apologies are accepted, my repentance is approved. The rest is a dream. It unreels like a spool of film; there is no stopping it. Aspinall promises to do everything he can to hurry my meeting with General von Svestrom, and I leave him, knowing that not even documentary proof that I am Rabbi Ben Ezra will deflect him now.

When I told Franticek what I was planning to do he turned his back on me without a word. I'm not afraid of him ratting on me to Aspinall. For one thing he doesn't speak English; for another he'll never mention my name to anyone again if he can help it.

I don't care enough about Paul or Dieter to tell them anything, but I feel I must explain it to Abri. He says, "It's the right thing for you, Tyl. I'm glad," but he looks sick.

For Michael there is another letter. I don't feel too guilty about him, though, for the truth is—and Michael in his honest moments could always be made to admit this—that when an actor says I love you to someone else, he is two-timing himself.

Migaud says, "*Quel dommage.* I hope you will be very happy." But later in the evening he sends around one of his rough trade boys with a present for me: the smallest and saddest of his Picassos, his favorite and mine, El Loco, the drawing of a mad beggar in a dusty Spanish street.

The incomparable Aspinall does it in less than a week. He even lent me a jeep and a driver to take me where I would willingly walk barefoot over hot coals.

He came downstairs to see me off, terribly nice and earnest. (Heart of a gentleman, brains of a boy scout.)

"I know it wasn't an easy decision for you, Tyl. But I'm sure you're doing the right thing. Families should be together."

The driver lets in the clutch. I remember suddenly that I've left all of my papers, drawings, notebooks, diaries upstairs. I can't even remember all there is: five-o'clock-in-the-morning insomniac scribbles, a lot of them, for which I don't particularly want to be held responsible. Do I mind enough to go back and get them? Not worth it. Let's go.

Aspinall and I shake hands. He says, "I know this is right, Tyl. It must be. This is the first time since I've known you that I have seen you laugh."

Postscript by Captain William Aspinall:
"God damn and blast the lying little bastard straight to hell!"